have a nice life

(play)

by
Scarlett MacDougal

AlloyBooks

ALLOYBOOKS

Published by the Penguin Group

Penguin Putnam Books for Young Readers,

345 Hudson Street, New York, New York 10014, U.S.A.

Penguin Books Ltd, 27 Wrights Lane, London W8 5TZ, England

Penguin Books Australia Ltd, Ringwood, Victoria, Australia

Penguin Books Canada Ltd, 10 Alcorn Avenue, Toronto, Ontario, Canada M4V 3B2

Penguin Books (N.Z.) Ltd, 182-190 Wairau Road, Auckland 10, New Zealand

Penguin Books Ltd, Registered Offices: Harmondsworth, Middlesex, England

Published by Puffin Books,

a division of Penguin Putnam Books for Young Readers, 2000

1 3 5 7 9 10 8 6 4 2

Produced by 17th Street Productions,

an Alloy Online, Inc. company

33 West 17th Street

New York, NY 10011

ISBN 0-14-131021-9

Printed in the United States of America

For the original Ozzy

(1)

(Lucy Skywalker)

Clarence Terence parked his motorcycle in front of the Madizen Wiskarma Yoga Center. He was late. The seven A.M. rise-and-shine class was already under way.

Clarence slipped into the back of the studio, unrolled his purple sticky mat, and began the downward-facing dog pose, which is a fancy way of saying that his hands and feet were on the floor while his butt was stuck way up in the air. What a way to start the day.

If yoga was good enough for Madonna, it was certainly good enough for him. But who really wanted to do the monkey pose or a headstand at this hour of the morning? In fact, wherever she was, Madonna was probably still sound asleep.

The only reason he had come to yoga was to try to relax his mind, but he couldn't stop thinking about Zola Mitchell. He wasn't thinking about her *that* way. He was

1

worried about her. Like a father. Well, more like a mother. A fairy godmother, to be exact.

The whole thing really should have been easy. Come down to Earth to show four cute Madison, Wisconsin, girls their futures and complete his karmic destiny at the same time. Simple, right? But what Clarence had learned in the past twenty-four hours—which included a harrowing high school senior prom and an exhausting postprom sleep-over party—was that nothing was ever simple.

He had met up with Zola Mitchell, Min Weinstock, Olivia Dawes, and Sally Wilder right after their senior prom and shown each girl her future, *personally* escorting her forward in time. And what had he gotten for his trouble? One giant hassle after another. You'd think they would be thrilled to receive a visit from him, their fairy godmother, and actually get to see their own futures. Who wouldn't want to see what happens to them ten years from now? But these girls were all about bitching and moaning, without one iota of gratitude.

Of course their futures weren't great, but that was the whole point.

Clarence had come to realize that no matter how many light-years you traveled away from Earth or how much wisdom and perspective you gathered, it was still never enough to understand women. Especially teenage women.

If the angel in *It's a Wonderful Life* had to deal with

Georgette Bailey instead of George Bailey, it would have been a whole different movie. He would have had to hang around, flapping his wings in the breeze, waiting for Georgette to put on her makeup and check herself out in the mirror to see if she looked fat. If Yoda had to deal with *Lucy* Skywalker instead of Luke, they never would have gotten around to *Episode 1: The Phantom Menace*. But then again, that might not have been such a bad thing.

"Now we're going to move into the goddess," the yoga instructor announced. Her voice was so high and perky, it was giving Clarence a headache.

"Clarence, would you like to be our goddess today?" she asked, walking lightly across the wooden floor toward him.

The other women in the class giggled.

"What?" Clarence asked, putting his hands on his hips and glaring at them. "You never saw a fine black man do the goddess pose before?"

The teacher began to guide him into the pose.

"Stretch your arms out like this," she said, lifting Clarence's arms so they stretched out like airplane wings on either side of his body. "Now bend your elbows, keeping your upper arms at a ninety-degree angle from your torso, hands on either side of your ears. Keep them parallel, palms facing each other. Now bend your knees slightly. Your heels should remain on the floor throughout the pose. Keep your body as vertical as possible. Soften your gaze, quiet your hearing, relax your jaw. Breathe evenly and comfortably through your nose."

Clarence did as he was told, wobbling slightly on his mat. Yoga looked so simple and easy on those badly produced yoga programs on local cable channels, but it took a lot of concentration and strength. Clarence thought he was in pretty good shape, but he could feel sweat beading on his forehead. What he really needed right now was an iced latte.

"Widen your stance," the teacher instructed. She smelled like feet. Clarence held his breath so he wouldn't have to smell her. "That way you'll have more balance," the teacher continued. "Feel your feet, rooted in the ground, your body rising up like a strong tree. And *breathe*."

Clarence did his best. He felt powerful in the pose. He felt like Diana, the mythical Greek goddess of the hunt.

Zola reminded him of Diana the huntress. She was so strong willed and determined to get what she wanted. Although what she wanted happened to be Evan Fell, her ex-boyfriend, who was now dating Claudia Choney. Claudia was top of the class gradewise, but her morals were rock-bottom. During the prom Zola had caught Evan and Claudia practically having sex in the back of the limo that was supposed to have taken *her* to the prom. It was like *Cinderhella:* Evan, the prince, ending up with the skankiest, most hideous stepsister in the back of the pumpkin carriage instead of with Zola.

Evan was a good guy, Clarence had to admit, but he wasn't the only fish in the sea. And if Evan was that easily led astray, he really wasn't worth the fuss. But Zola didn't see it that way. She was psychotically jealous of Claudia. Everything Zola did or thought or said had something to do with making Claudia pay the price for stealing Evan away. It was as if Zola had confused love with hate. She loved Evan, so she was determined to hate Claudia. Jealousy makes people ugly, and Zola's future wasn't pretty.

Not that Zola grew warts and a lumpy nose and a hunched back in the future. In fact, for now, the future Zola was a model. But not the kind of model she wanted to be. She posed for sleazy men's magazines, wearing practically nothing. And Evan wound up married to Claudia.

The more Clarence thought about Zola's life, the more it seemed like an episode of *90210*. He made a mental note to put in a call to FOX so he could pitch it as an idea for a new series. He could see himself at the meeting now, talking to the producers. He would tell them it was *The Breakfast Club* meets *The Joy Luck Club*. It could be called *The Joy Suck Club*. No, that sounded a little too porno.

The yoga instructor asked them to lie down on their

mats for deep relaxation. Clarence felt like a kindergarten student at nap time. It was nice.

Until he started to think about the girls again. Zola, Olivia, Min, Sally. He said their names and saw their faces over and over again in his mind.

Olivia. So eager to please everyone but herself, it was no wonder she ended up a flight attendant in the future, serving up chicken thumbs, cleaning up poopie diapers, and getting her butt pinched by fat old businessmen. Plus she was married to, and cheating on, Bill, her current sort-of boyfriend. Sort of in the sense that they sort of only ever fooled around in the storage closet in the biology lab, and sort of never once had a normal conversation, and had sort of never been on a single real date.

Min was the stable one in the group, which wasn't exactly saying much. In the future she ended up married to her boyfriend, Tobias, and Ozzy, his dog. Yes, married to both of them. Tobias was a freak who was more dog obsessed than the average healthy college boy should be. But he loved Min just as much as he loved his dog. Tobias was harmless, but Clarence thought the whole relationship was a little creepy.

And Sally. Clarence had a soft spot for Sally. He had been a lot like her when he was a kid—shy and always writing in a diary. And like him, she was sensitive. Clarence didn't think Sally's future was all that devastating. She ended up a teacher at La Follette High School, one of the very people they had all spent the past four years making fun of. Clarence had definitely seen worse. But when Sally saw what she would become, she was stricken, especially when she found out that she still lived at home with her mother. The way she saw it, she had no future.

Clarence hoped to teach the girls that in order to change their futures, they would have to change their presents. But not just the superficial things. Unfortunately, the girls had completely misunderstood him. They had expected to just put on new outfits, make a few phone calls, and change their lives in one day. They didn't understand that they would have to go a lot deeper than that. They had to start from the heart chakra, so to speak. They had to feel the change down to their solar plexuses.

Zola thought that the key to her happiness was getting even with Claudia. Olivia thought her problems could be solved by putting on a pair of Oliver Peoples eyeglasses and trying to act as smart as her SAT scores proved she actually was. Min was determined to dump Tobias and Ozzy so she wouldn't smell like dog for the rest of her life. And sweet, innocent Sally was convinced that all she had to do to not become a teacher was to have sex since it was obvious that none of the teachers she knew had ever had sex.

Clearly it wasn't that easy. And clearly Clarence and

7

the girls had a major communication problem. Either Clarence was going to have to start all over again or they were all going to have to go to some sort of group therapy workshop.

Clarence shifted his buttocks on the yoga mat, trying to relax. He was getting really worked up.

In the background of his thoughts he heard the teacher chant, "*Namaste*. I honor the place in you in which the entire universe dwells. I honor the place in you that is of love, of peace, of light, and of truth. When you are in that place in you and I am in that place in me, we are one."

Clarence breathed deeply and drifted back to his thoughts. If only he could be more *one* with the girls. If only he could get them to see things his way. Or maybe that was the wrong way of thinking about it. Maybe he needed to just *be*. Be present to them, there to help and guide them, without force. Like a good teacher, letting them learn for themselves and only intervening when absolutely necessary. He didn't know if he could do it, but he could try.

The thing was, he *enjoyed* intervening.

Zola, Min, Olivia, and Sally hadn't come with a manual, and Clarence hadn't counted on them being so difficult. But now something else had happened against his will—he cared about them. He had already gone well beyond the call of duty, even for a fairy godmother, but he really wanted to do a good job for the girls. Even if they were a pain in the you-know-what.

Clarence felt someone shake him and opened his eyes. A gigantic pregnant woman was standing over him. Clarence sat up quickly.

"You fell asleep," the woman said. "Your class is over. This is the eight o'clock Yoga Mama Lama class. Prenatal yoga."

Clarence got himself together and left. He strapped his yoga mat to the back of his motorcycle and took off through downtown Madison. As he cruised along the backstreets in the hip part of town, he felt panicky. Wasn't yoga supposed to give you a sense of inner peace?

Up ahead he spotted Bohème—the café-club-bistro where he'd gotten his great-grandnephew, Myles, a summer job. Myles was a bit of a slacker, and Clarence had promised the family that he would keep an eye on him. He was hoping he could get Myles together with the girls somehow. That way he could keep tabs on all five of them at once. Clarence pulled his motorcycle up to the curb and rolled his head around on his shoulders. He couldn't believe how stressed out he felt. Just a quick cappuccino and then he'd be off to find the girls.

② (Lenny Kravitz)

The first thing Zola wanted to do when she woke up that morning, besides pee, was talk to Evan. She had to see him. She had a million things she wanted to say. She was sorry she hadn't gone to the prom with him. She wished she hadn't put him down when he suggested that he pick her up in a limo. He had wanted the whole corsage, photos, dance-every-single-dance-together thing. She just wanted to go in a big group with her friends and make fun of people. She didn't know when Evan had turned into such a cornball. They had been dating for three and a half years, but suddenly it seemed like she didn't know him at all.

Then Claudia Choney managed to crawl her way into Zola's brain, and her stomach churned. She couldn't stand the thought of Claudia and Evan together. Touching each other. Kissing. What if they had actually had sex?

She knew she had been mean to Evan. She wasn't

even sure exactly why she had done what she'd done. She just wanted to show him she had a mind of her own. That not everything had to be so serious all the time. How could she have known that Evan would fall into Claudia Choney's clutches so easily?

Zola looked at her face in her bathroom mirror. She was so tall now, she had to hunch down to look in it. She had chin-length dark brown hair parted in the middle. She liked that; it was sort of mod. She had big brown eyes and high cheekbones. She remembered what Clarence had shown her the night before—her future as a skeevy bathing suit model. Her eyes looked sad then, and they looked sad now.

She could bet Claudia Choney's eyes looked happy. Claudia had won prom queen. Zola stuck out her tongue at the mirror. Maybe she should get it pierced like Claudia's. By now Claudia probably had *Evan* tattooed on her back.

Zola picked up the phone, dialed Evan's number, and listened to it ring three times. Unfortunately Evan's little brother, Todd, answered.

"Hello?" Todd said. "Hello?"

Zola didn't say anything.

"Hel-lo-o." Todd sighed deeply into the phone. "Speak, freak," he said.

Zola couldn't bring herself to say anything.

"Evan," Todd screamed at the top of his lungs. "There's a crazy prevert on the phone not saying anything, so it must be for you."

There was a banging sound, which Zola figured was the receiver of the mounted kitchen wall phone hitting the floor on its long spiral cord. Zola felt like she was the one hanging on a cord.

"Hello?" Evan said into the phone. "Hello?"

There was so much she wanted to tell Evan, but she suddenly realized it had to be in person. The sound of the dial tone woke her out of her trance, and she hung up the phone. She had to see him.

Zola showered and selected a pair of special make-up panties from her underwear drawer. She pulled on jeans, a T-shirt, and flip-flops and headed out to her car. But when she got to Evan's house, she was horrified to discover that she had pulled up right behind Claudia Choney's car. Claudia was there, in the house!

Zola's eyes welled up with tears. What was going on? She had cried more in the past two days than she had in the past ten years combined. She had to pull herself together. She wrapped her arms around herself. The only thing that would make her feel better would be to kick Claudia's ass. But what could she do? I should slash her tires, Zola thought. She actually sat in the car for a few minutes, contemplating slashing Claudia's tires. She went so far as to look through her glove compartment for a sharp object, but all she found was a small pair of scissors from her manicure kit. She couldn't very well slash a tire with nail scissors.

Just then Clarence Terence pulled up on his motorcycle. Zola rolled down her window.

"Yes?" she said.

"I have something for you," Clarence said.

"What, some more bad news about my future?" Zola asked. Actually, she was glad to see him. Maybe he could tell her how to get Evan back.

Clarence lifted up an enormous bucket of red liquid.

"Jesus, Lenny, what the hell is that?" Zola asked. The girls had started calling Clarence Lenny because they thought he looked exactly like Lenny Kravitz, especially with his penchant for playing the guitar and wearing fabulous custom-made leather outfits. He just didn't seem like a Clarence. He was a Lenny.

"My name isn't Lenny," Clarence said. "And unfortunately this is not a bucket of Bloody Marys. What do you think it is?"

"I have no idea," Zola said. If Lenny wasn't going to be helpful, she wished he would just leave her alone.

"It's pig's blood," Clarence said. "I thought you might want to pour it on Claudia's head. Just like that fabulous scene in *Carrie.*"

Zola looked at him in disbelief. Was he serious? Did he really think she should do that?

"I mean," Clarence continued, "you missed your opportunity to dump pig's blood on her head at the prom, but there's no time like the present. I know it's been *done,* but you've got to admit it's got a certain retro kitsch charm."

"You're sick," Zola said. "That is the grossest thing I've ever heard." Although she was beginning to wonder if it wasn't also the best idea Lenny had had yet.

"My point is that you're not doing yourself any favors by brooding in your car outside Evan's house like a psycho stalker," Clarence said. "Do the words *restraining order* mean anything to you?"

"I should take out a restraining order against you," Zola said, pouting.

"Who ever heard of anyone taking out a restraining order against their fairy godmother?" Clarence said, putting his hands on his hips. "Do you think Cinderella would have snagged the prince if she'd taken a restraining order out on her fairy godmother? What's wrong with you? Where's the gratitude?"

"Okay, okay," Zola said. "But next time leave the visual effects at home, please. What are you going to do with all that pig's blood, anyway? It's disgusting."

"I guess I'll just have to drive around and look for someone wearing a fur coat," Clarence said. He sighed. "But look at all the leather I've got on. I suppose that's a bit hypocritical."

Zola laughed in spite of herself. For a fairy godmother, he looked pretty hot in his tight blue leather pants, sitting on that bike. She *was* pretty lucky to have him.

And Zola knew Clarence was right—she had to get out of there. It would be humiliating if Evan or Claudia saw her sitting outside in her car like a hopeless loser. She felt her heartbeat speed up just thinking about it. Oh, Claudia was going to pay for this. She was going to *pay, pay, pay.*

③

(Upward and Outward)

Incredibly tense, Sally wrote in her diary. *I feel incredibly tense. Everything is going wrong. I'm going to be a teacher, but I want to be a writer. I'm going to live with my mother, but I want to live with a beautiful man and hold hands in front of the fire. I know I will never find anyone to lose my virginity to. I'll be a virgin for the rest of my life. And it's impossible to relax, knowing Lenny could pop in at any moment.*

She put down her pen and wrapped her bathrobe more tightly around herself. What if he showed up sometime when she was naked?

She put her feet up on the couch and opened the book she was reading, called *How to Meet a Man Fast.* **Look at yourself right now,** she read in chapter one. **Are you lying in bed? Are you lazing on the couch?** Sally nodded to herself. She *was* lazing on her couch. She read on. **Now, look around the room. Do you see any handsome, eligible men in your house?**

16

Sally shook her head no. She had to admit there were no handsome, eligible men in her house. There weren't any men at all in her house.

She read on. ***The worst thing a single girl can do is stay at home. You will never, ever meet a man lying around your house, reading this book,*** the book said. ***Every hour you stay at home reading is another hour you are giving up on your own future. You should be out in cafés, at wine tastings, singles dances, dating services, town meetings, Club Med, sports events, parties, beaches, parks, bookstores, walking tours, local cultural happenings, museums, houses of worship, coed health clubs, in-line skating, cigar bars. . . .*** The words on the page began to squiggle. Sally suddenly became so dizzy her eyes started to roll back in her head, and she began to sweat. She really couldn't imagine herself at a cigar bar. She couldn't even stand the smell of cigars, and the thought of trying to smoke one made her want to gag. She was completely doomed.

She reached for the remote control on the coffee table. Maybe if she watched TV for a little while, it would quiet her thoughts. She turned on the local news. The book said she should keep up with current events so she would seem intelligent on dates.

"And now, onward and upward," the newscaster said. "Or should we say, upward and outward. Victoria's Secret has come out with the Aquabra, a new *water-filled* push-up bra. Dana Davis, our reporter in the field, is there to find out how it is holding up, so to speak. Dana?"

Dana Davis came on the screen, with one hand over her ear and her other hand holding a microphone. "Thanks, Richard," she said.

Sally gasped. It was the woman who had interviewed her against her will the day before outside the dressing room at Victoria's Secret. This was worse than any nightmare. The salesgirl had talked her into trying on the bra, and then that stupid newswoman had accosted her when she stepped out of the dressing room to look at herself in the mirror. It had been such an unbelievably embarrassing episode, Sally had tried to block it out of her life altogether. She hadn't even written about it in her diary. But now there she was on the TV screen, wearing that obscene push-up bra under her T-shirt and staring into the camera. What if someone from school was watching? "No," Sally told the television, as if she could stop it from happening.

"What's your name?" Dana Davis asked TV Sally. She held the microphone up to TV Sally's face.

"Uh, Sally Wilder," TV Sally said into the mike. Sally sat on the couch with her hands over her face. It was too awful to watch.

"What does your boyfriend say when you wear the new water-filled bra?" Dana Davis asked.

"I, uh, I don't have a boyfriend. I mean there's Dean, but he's never seen my bra." The camera panned down to a close-up of Sally's chest. It was already big, but it appeared huge in the bra, like giant mutant breasts created by some dirty old scientist.

"Well, there you have it, Madison, Wisconsin," Dana Davis announced. "Sally Wilder may not have a boyfriend yet, but with her new Aquabra she's sure to get one soon enough."

Sally had heard that in times of terrible trauma, people sometimes become very calm. People in plane crashes or car accidents go into shock, causing them to react in a cool and collected manner. That's what was happening to her. Instead of completely freaking out, she just sat calmly on the couch and opened her diary.

The worst thing that has ever happened to me just happened, she wrote.

The phone rang, and she answered it calmly. It was Min. "Sally, are you aware your breasts were just on national television?" Min asked.

"I was wearing a T-shirt, and I don't think it's national; I think it's local," Sally said.

"Oh, well, in that case it's fine," Min said sarcastically.

"Nice tits, Sal," Min's boyfriend, Tobias, shouted in the background.

Sally's vision had gone blurry, and her mouth was dry.

She sat down on the floor even though there was an arm-chair a foot away from where she was standing.

"Seriously, it's not the end of the world, Sally," Min said.

Sally's call waiting went off. She said good-bye to Min and answered it. It was Olivia. "Why didn't you tell us you were going to be on TV?" She sounded impressed. Typical Olivia.

Then the call waiting went off again, and Sally hung up on Olivia. It was Zola. "Wow, Sally," she said. "You're the one who should be a bikini model. I mean, shit—I'd do you!"

Sally cringed, remembering what had happened with Zola at the prom. They had been in the school parking lot, comparing notes on how horrendously the night was going, when out of the blue Zola had kissed her. Really kissed her. Of course Zola was drunk at the time, but Sally couldn't stop wondering what it had all meant. Zola didn't even seem to remember it.

"Look, Sal," Zola said, her voice suddenly gentle—the tone she usually reserved for her younger brother, Nathaniel. "If you need me to fend off the paparazzi for you, I will. Okay? Are you all right?"

"Hmn," Sally said. Her call waiting went off again. "I'll talk to you later," she mumbled, and hung up on Zola.

"Hello?" she said to the next caller. There was a

snigger on the end of the line. It sounded like a group of eleven-year-old boys. "Boobies!" someone shouted. And then they hung up.

Within minutes Sally had gotten a call from her grandpa Joe, asking her when she had decided to become a prostitute, and fifteen anonymous obscene calls. The phone wouldn't stop ringing. Finally she just let the machine pick up.

"Hi, Sally, this is Dean," she heard him say into the machine. "Uh, I'd really rather you didn't, uh, talk about me on television again. I've gotten a lot of calls, and it's been very embarrassing."

"I'm sorry," Sally said to the answering machine. She could tell by the tone of Dean's voice that he would never go out with her again. Dean didn't want any skeletons in his closet. He wanted to be a famous actor, and he probably thought dating her would be a bad career move. Like dating a porn star.

Then there was a message from Clarence. "Don't worry, Sally. You know what they say. There's no such thing as bad publicity."

Sally liked Lenny a lot. Probably too much, in fact. But she had to admit that that was the stupidest thing she had ever heard.

(Cozy)

Min turned off the TV in her family's rumpus room. Tobias couldn't stop howling with laughter and slapping his knees, and it was really beginning to annoy her. She hated it when he made fun of her friends. And she felt truly terrible for Sally.

"Cut it out, Tobias," Min said.

Tobias made a tiny effort to stifle his laughter. He scooped Ozzy, his Yorkshire terrier, up off the floor and put him on Min's father's pool table. Ozzy loved the green felt tabletop. He thought it was grass. He walked around, sniffing the whole thing, and then scratched at one of the corner pockets.

"He must feel like he's on his own private indoor field," Tobias mused, staring lovingly at Ozzy. "Maybe I should get a pool table for him."

"You don't even have an apartment and you're thinking about getting a pool table?" Min asked.

"I mean when I get an apartment."

22

"What are you going to do, Tobias?" Min asked. "You know you can't stay here. You're going to have to figure out someplace else to go."

"That's true," Tobias said. "It's kind of hard to sleep in a room with *that,* anyway." He pointed to Min's mother's latest handcrafted creation. "What the hell *is* that?"

Min couldn't even begin to explain. You've heard of a tea cozy? Well, this was a vacuum cleaner cozy. It was like an enormous rabbit puppet covering the upright vacuum cleaner standing in the corner, with a big stuffed head, a gingham dress, and a white pinafore. It was indescribably absurd looking. Min's mother was really into rabbits lately.

"But it's worth having to wake up and look at the vacuum rabbit because I get to be near you," Tobias said. He buried his face in Min's neck and growled like a happy puppy into her ear.

Min sighed, exasperated. This whole thing was a huge mess. Just when she was absolutely determined to break up with him, Tobias showed up at her door, homeless, because his college roommates had kicked him out. He had spent last night in the rumpus room without her parents knowing. Not only hadn't she managed to break up with him, now they were living together.

Ozzy looked very much like he was about to pee, sniffing and circling in an urgent manner. Just in time Min grabbed him and put him down on the newspaper they had laid out. It was one thing if her father caught her housing a college boy, but it was another thing altogether if his favorite thing in the world, his pool table, got peed on.

Her father was a rabbi, the least-strict rabbi you've ever met. He let Min drive his car and stay out late and do just about anything she wanted, including party with her friends down in the rumpus room until all hours of the evening. But he wasn't crazy about his daughter dating a man who was already in college. Min wondered what her father would think if he knew Tobias and Ozzy were living in his house!

Min didn't even know what she thought about it. There were good things about Tobias, even if he acted like a jerk a lot of the time. He could really make her laugh, for one thing. Then she remembered the future Lenny had shown her. She was married to Tobias, and they were both fat and miserable and going to a marriage counselor.

"Tobias, Lady M doesn't think we should go out anymore," Min said, using the special name she called herself when she was dealing with something serious. She couldn't believe the words were coming out of her mouth. "Clarence Terence said . . ." She stopped herself. He would never understand about Clarence.

"What?" Tobias asked. "Who is Clarence Terence?"

"No one," Min said.

"Honey, I'll kill myself if you leave me for this Clarence guy. Don't do this to me, Min. You can't break up with me.

I love you so much. Please, honey." He got down on his knees in front of her.

"No, you don't understand. I'm not seeing Lenny. . . ."

"I love you, Min," Tobias said. He put his cheek against her stomach. She touched the top of his head lovingly. She suddenly couldn't remember why she was breaking up with him.

Min heard footsteps upstairs. "Min, are you down there?" her father called from the top of the stairs.

"I'll be right up, Dad," she said nervously.

Then she heard footsteps coming down the stairs. Tobias stood up. There was nowhere for him to hide. Why had she done this? Min was crazy to think she could get away with this.

Her father appeared. "Min? Tobias?" he said, obviously surprised. Min wasn't supposed to be alone in the house with Tobias. And he wasn't wearing any shoes, which seemed odd for some reason.

"Dad . . ."

"Let me," Tobias said, putting out his hand. "Hello, Rabbi Weinstock, it's nice to see you again." Min's father shook Tobias's hand and seemed to relax a little. Min's eyes darted around the room, looking for Ozzy. Miraculously, he had decided to sleep under the couch. "Sir, I would just like to say that I have the best of intentions toward your daughter."

A small smile came to the rabbi's lips. "Oh?" he said. "I'm glad to hear that."

"Min and I have been dating for quite a while, and I regret that I haven't gotten to know you and your wife better," Tobias said. "I hope you'll give me the chance to prove myself to you, sir."

Min and her father both looked surprised to see how nice and polite Tobias was being. Min could tell her father was thinking that perhaps he had misjudged Tobias.

"Well, Mrs. Weinstock and I would certainly like to get to know you better," Min's father said.

"I think you'll find I'm quite a mensch, sir."

He was right about that, Min thought. Tobias *was* a mensch. But he could also be a real pain in the ass. A surprisingly lovable, funny pain in the ass.

Min's father laughed. "Call me Steve," he said.

"Dad, Tobias has nowhere to stay for the next few days. Is it okay if he stays here?" She couldn't believe she was asking this.

Her father paused. "Sure," he said. "I don't see why not. As long as he promises to wear shoes most of the time, he's in for the night before eleven, and"—he gave Min a stern look—*"he stays down here."*

"Of course, sir," Tobias said, clearing his throat.

Min wondered if he could hear Ozzy snoring.

5

(Futureshok)

Olivia lay on her bed, looking at Holden's phone number on the back of a Borders bookmark. The first three numbers were 666. That was so cool. Even his phone number was cool.

And she loved the idea that she had met him in a bookstore. It was so mature and serious. She couldn't wait to say to people, "Oh, we met in a bookstore." It sounded so much better than, "We met in biology class," or, "We met in PE." She wished she knew Holden's last name so she could see how it sounded with Olivia. She figured it probably wasn't Caulfield.

The sun looked beautiful filtering through the curtains her mother had made. It was just about the only domestic-y thing her mother had ever done. She had taken Indian saris, cut them in half, and hemmed them.

Olivia looked at the pile of books next to her on the bed. She had promised herself she would study today. It was Senior Monday. Senior Monday was the Monday after the prom, and even though it was a regular school day, it was tradition at La Follette for all the seniors to stay home.

Even science nerds like Bill stayed home. Bill. She had promised to meet him in the bio lab before first period on Tuesday. She really didn't want to think about that right now.

Olivia went to her desk and turned on her computer to see if Holden had sent her an e-mail. She signed on to AOL. There was nothing. Then the instant message box popped up in the top-left corner of her screen. It wasn't Zola, Sally, or Min. It was someone named Futureshok.

Hey, O.D.onlove, Futureshok wrote.

Olivia typed, *Do I know you?* and hit reply.

Yes, Futureshok wrote.

Olivia smiled. *Holden?*

What are you holden??? Futureshok wrote.

Maybe I'd like to be holden you tight, Olivia wrote.

Shouldn't you be holden your homework? Futureshok responded. *As far as I can remember, you still have to write one more extra-credit paper for English if you want a shot at valedictorian.*

Olivia stopped smiling. It wasn't Holden. It was Clarence Terence, checking up on her.

Lenny? she typed.

A digital image of Clarence wearing a red, white, and blue hat and pointing his finger Uncle Sam–style filled up the screen. The words *I Want You* flashed across the bottom.

Olivia laughed. He was so corny. And she would never get over how much he looked like Lenny Kravitz. She felt like she had Lenny Kravitz for a fairy godmother. She, Zola, Min, and Sally had promised not to call him Lenny anymore because it pissed him off so much, but none of them had been able to do it.

Lenny, dear, Olivia wrote, *don't you have anything else to do?*

Just thought you needed a little hand-Holden, Clarence wrote.

Hey, Lenny, any advice? Olivia wrote.

Yeah. Don't talk to strangers on the Internet. And don't call me Lenny.

With that, he was gone.

⑥

(Crossing the Street)

Olivia, Min, Zola, and Sally got in their cars and met up on the Isthmus in downtown Madison. Sally had been desperate to get out of the house and away from her ringing phone. Min was free because Tobias had a class. Olivia had given up on her English paper. And Zola was willing to do anything just to keep her mind off killing Claudia.

They got frozen mochaccinos and walked for a while.

"I feel like our whole lives are turned around," Olivia said. "We were just going around minding our own businesses and some motorcycle-riding Martian freak Lenny Kravitz look-alike from outer space barges into our lives to mess with our heads. Maybe this whole thing is just one big mind game."

"How do we know he's even right?" Zola asked. "Maybe he's got our futures all wrong."

"It's not like he showed us any ID," Sally said.

Min looked at Sally and laughed. "ID?" she said. "That's the most ridiculous thing I've ever heard. A man takes us flying on his motorcycle and shows us our futures and you want us to ID him?"

All the girls laughed except for Sally.

"Why don't we ask to see his diploma to make sure he graduated from an accredited fairy godmother school?" Min said.

"Piss off," Sally said.

"Sally, you've already changed," Min said. "Just *wanting* to get laid has turned you into a bit of a potty mouth."

"All right, leave her alone," Zola said. "The point is, Lenny could be wrong. And even if he's right, remember what he said? Just one thing could change our futures. So, if we all cross the street right now, even though we weren't intending to, our lives will change forever. Come on." Zola started crossing the street, and the other girls followed.

"Why did the girls cross the road?" Min asked.

"To change their futures," Olivia answered. "Wouldn't it have been cool if we all got hit by a car and became paralyzed or something and you turned out to be right?"

"Oh yeah, Olivia. It would be really cool to get hit by a car and be paralyzed," Sally said, shaking her head in wonder at her friend's stupidity.

"Hey, what's this?" Min said. They were standing in

front of a little basement storefront with a sign in the window that said Madame Nemchineva, Fortune-teller. A rail-thin woman in a green housedress, her gray hair tied into a bun, sat on a folding chair in the window and made a beckoning gesture at them with her bony finger.

"We must have walked past here a hundred times. Did you ever notice this before?" Olivia asked.

The other girls shook their heads.

A boy about their age in board shorts and no shirt walked by and did a double take when he saw Sally. "Don't I know you?" he asked.

Sally put her chin down and shook her head.

"Yeah, I know you from somewhere," he said. He looked her up and down. Sally turned bright red.

Zola stepped forward. "This is Sally," she said, sort of shoving Sally toward the boy. "And you are?"

"What is this, an arranged marriage?" Min said, trying to come to Sally's rescue but just making things worse. Sally felt like she was about to pass out.

"I know!" the boy said. "You're the girl in the bra. On TV today." He looked right at her chest. "I knew you looked familiar. I never forget a face," he said, still staring at her chest.

"Look, Sally has a fan," Olivia said.

Sally crossed her arms in front of her.

"Come on," Zola said, grabbing the back of Sally's

T-shirt and pulling her toward the steps to Madame Nemchineva's, with Min and Olivia right behind them.

Madame Nemchineva rose from her chair and opened the door for them. "Vhat beautiful young ladies you are," she said in a Russian accent.

Sally looked all around the storefront. It didn't look like the room of a fortune-teller. There was lime green wall-to-wall carpet, two folding chairs and a small card table, and a yellow curtain hiding some sort of back area.

"Vhat can I do for you?" Madame Nemchineva said.

None of the girls said anything. Sally was still fuming from what had just happened with the obnoxious boy. Her fan.

Madame Nemchineva put her fingers to her temples. "I can see you are upset about something," she said to Sally.

"How much is it?" Min asked.

"Twenty dollars for each beautiful girl," the fortune-teller said.

Sally blushed. Whenever anyone said she was beautiful, even a million-year-old Russian woman, it made her blush.

"Excuse us for one minute," Min said, grabbing her friends into a sort of huddle. "I think we should do it," she whispered.

"Eighty bucks is a lot of money," Olivia said. "What if she's a fake?"

"I don't want to do it. You three can," Sally said. The last thing in the world she wanted was to have to see her future again. How masochistic could her friends be? Enough was enough. She felt absolutely no need or desire to go through that hell again. Bad enough she had Clarence Terence leaving messages on her answering machine about the push-up bra incident. She wasn't going to *pay* to be tortured.

"Maybe just one of us should do it," Zola said.

The others agreed. But who should it be?

"It seems to me," Zola said, "that Min's situation is the most crucial. And the most fixable."

"Thanks a lot," Min said.

"You know what I mean. You really have to get rid of that loser, especially now that he's living in your house. What are you going to do, Min? Why don't we each chip in five dollars and get Min's fortune told?" Zola said.

Zola, Olivia, and Sally looked at Min expectantly.

"Fine, it will be me," Min said.

"Vell?" Madame Nemchineva said, sounding annoyed.

The girls all took out wallets and ponied up their share. "I'd like my fortune told," Min said.

⑦

(Leetle Ones)

Madame Nemchineva drew back the curtain to expose a room with walls that were painted red and a low round table surrounded by cushions on a Persian carpet. On the table was a deck of tarot cards cut into three piles.

"Please sit yourselves," Madame Nemchineva said.

The girls sat around the table and looked around at the strange room. In one corner was a shelf with crystals and bottles of herbs. The walls were covered with pictures of swamis and women with scarves on their heads. But most surprising was a framed poster of Ricky Martin.

"Uh, excuse me, Madame Nemchineva," Zola said, suppressing a laugh. "Why do you have a picture of Ricky Martin? Do you channel him or something?"

"First of all," Madame Nemchineva said, lowering herself to her cushion on the floor. Everyone listened to the sound of a thousand bones creak. "You cannot channel ze spirit of a person who is living. Zat poster is zere because

35

my niece is a big Ricky Martin fan. And second of all, my name is not Madame Nemchineva. It is Rose Schwartz."

"Oh, I'm sorry," Zola said. "The sign said Madame Nemchineva."

"Yes, I know," Rose Schwartz said. "Madame Nemchineva looks better on a sign." She turned to Min, who was sitting to her right, and took Min's hands in her own bony ones. "Now, vhat is your name. . . . No, don't tell me. It begins with a *va* sound."

"No," Min said, looking nervously at her friends. "It's Min. A *ma* sound."

"No," Rose Schwartz said.

"Actually it's really Wilamina," Min said.

"Yes, Vilamina. *Va.* Rose Schwartz is never wrong," Rose said. "So tell me, Vilamina. Vhat is your question?"

Suddenly there was a loud high-pitched wail coming from somewhere in the room. Sally started to panic. It was clearly some sort of angry spirit. The ghost of Ricky Martin's great-grandfather or some such. She wanted to get the hell out of there.

"Please vait a moment," Rose said, and went to a tremendous amount of effort to stand all the way up again. She went behind a Chinese screen and came back carrying a tray with five paper cups and a teapot in the shape of a cow.

She poured tea for everyone except Sally, who had

no intention of drinking some strange witch's brew.

"Lenny doesn't serve tea," Olivia whispered to Zola.

"Who is zis Lenny?" Rose asked.

"Uh, he's a friend of ours," Zola said.

"A troublemaker, no?" Rose said.

"Well, that's sort of my question," Min said.

"Shhh," Rose said, putting a finger to her lips. She turned over the top card of one of the stacks to reveal a picture of a man wearing a crown and a robe. He was sitting on a throne. The card was called the Emperor. "There is an older man in your life who has control over you," Rose announced.

The girls nodded solemnly.

She turned over the top card of the middle stack. It was a picture of a court jester wearing a hat with three points. It was the Fool card. "He is wiser than he appears, he makes you laugh, and he's not so bad in ze sack."

Min choked on a sip of tea.

Rose turned over the top card of the third stack to reveal a naked couple holding hands with a beautiful beach scene behind them. "Ze Lovers!" Rose exclaimed. "My dear, zis may come as a surprise to you, but I believe you are soon to be vid child. You may even be pregnant right now."

"What!" Zola said.

Rose put her fingers to her temples and closed her eyes. "Yes!" she said. "I see leetle ones!"

"Ones?" Min asked, horrified.

"You are definitely pregnant," Rose said.

Olivia put her arm around Min, who was as pale as a ghost. Sally was about to go into full-fledged shock.

"Zis Lenny. He is ze father? No?"

"No!" Min shook her head. Now she was totally confused. Did Rose know what she was talking about? She was wrong about Lenny being the father, that was for sure. But was she right about everything else? Her mind raced, trying to remember all the times she and Tobias had had sex since her last period. They had been careful to use a condom every time. The only time they hadn't been that careful was last night! She had sneaked down to the rec room to bring Tobias a cup of hot chocolate and they had done it on the pullout sofa bed. She had been too nervous to go back upstairs to her room to get a condom and risk waking her parents. But they had been pretty careful, anyway—there was no way she could be pregnant. This was the worst thing that could happen to her.

"And it is definitely more than one," Rose said.

"What's more than one?" Min asked.

"I see more than one inside of you. You have twins. Maybe even triplets."

Rose reached over and grabbed one of Min's long dark hairs and pulled it right out of her head. She took the pink plastic daisy ring off Min's finger and tied the ring to the hair. Min sat there miserably while Rose dangled the daisy ring over Min's stomach to see if the baby was a boy or a girl.

"If it goes back and forth, it's a boy; if it goes in circles, it's a girl," Rose said.

They all stared at the makeshift pendulum. It didn't go back and forth or in circles. It didn't move.

"You see," Rose said, satisfied. "It's both. A boy and a girl." She gave Min back her ring.

Zola and Olivia stood and helped Min up to her feet. Then they had to help Sally, who looked like she was in a trance.

"Gratuities kindly accepted," they heard Rose call behind them as they rushed out onto the street.

(First Response)

The first thing Min did when they got out on the sidewalk was throw up. The girls stood around the small puddle of vomit, staring at it.

"Well," Zola said. "There you have it. The proof is in the pudding."

At the sound of the word *pudding,* Sally threw up, too.

"Sally, there's no way you're pregnant, too, is there?" Olivia said.

"I think what we need is to go somewhere and just calmly sit down and talk about all this," Zola said.

"I really need to sit down," Sally agreed. "I feel dizzy."

"How do you think *I* feel?" Min said.

"Everything's going to be okay," Zola said as they started walking to find a place where they could sit and talk.

Zola could be surprisingly soothing at just the right moments. Those five simple words calmed everyone down. Everything *was* going to be okay.

Zola herself had always wondered what she would do if it happened to her. If she accidentally became pregnant. She always had safe sex, but still, accidents could happen and it was good to be prepared with a plan. Life was full of surprises. But she was glad it wasn't her little surprise, that's for sure.

The girls sat down at a table outside Bohème, which was almost too cool for their purposes. They didn't care where they were as long as they could sit, talk, and drink coffee.

"Bonjour, mademoiselles," said a ridiculously good-looking boy wearing an apron and a beret over his short dreadlocks. "Are you ready to order?"

"*Sí*, señor," Olivia said, flirting. The waiter looked like Lenny, only younger. He was definitely hot.

Zola gave her a sharp how-could-you-even-think-of-flirting-at-a-time-like-this? look.

"*Sí*, señor?" The waiter laughed. "That's Spanish. Wrong language."

"*Excusez moi,*" Zola told him. She didn't care how good-looking he was. They had business to attend to.

They ordered coffee for Zola, Olivia, and Sally and a mineral water for Min. "I should probably cut down on caffeine now or something," Min said. "For the baby."

"Now, wait a minute," Zola said. "When was your last period?"

Min took a small Hello Kitty date book out of her pocketbook. She turned some pages and counted some days. "It's been about a month. I should be getting it any day now."

"So you're not late at all?" Zola asked.

Min shook her head. "I can't believe this," she said, putting her head in her hands. "Lady M is not amused. And why did we have to sit at this table?" She pointed across the street to a clothing store called From Here to Maternity. The window was filled with pregnant mannequins wearing hideous dresses. "I suppose we'll have to go in there and get me something to wear for graduation."

"Well, this is one way to change our futures," Olivia said. "We could all get pregnant. What do you think Lenny would think of that? Our futures would be different, all right. Hey, Min, you could name it Lenny if it's a boy and Lenore if it's a girl."

"This isn't a joke, Olivia," Min said.

"Sorry," Olivia mumbled, hurt. Of course, she felt sorry for Min, but a tiny deep-down part of her was also a little bit jealous for some reason. If she were the one pregnant, certain things about her life would be decided without her having to think about it. In a way it would almost be a load off her mind. She could keep the baby and go to school part-time. She would never become a stewardess because she'd have to be home to look after her child when it came home from school.

The waiter brought their drinks and just stood there, grinning at them in an impossibly cute way. This was just about the only time in history that the girls could have cared less that there was a stud in their midst.

"Au revoir," Zola said as obnoxiously as possible. The waiter stopped smiling and went away.

"What am I going to do?" Min said. "I have to tell Tobias and—"

"I don't know if that's such a good idea," Zola interrupted. "You need some time to think. Don't forget you were just about to break up with him. This is going to screw all that up. He may try to pressure you into doing something dumb. I think you should decide what *you* want to do *before* you tell him."

Olivia nodded solemnly. "I agree with Zola," she said. She took a sip of her coffee and tried not to make a face. She absolutely detested the taste of coffee, but she didn't want to seem immature by ordering hot chocolate.

"I know one thing," Min said. "I definitely want an epidural."

"What are you talking about?" Olivia asked.

"An epidural," Min said. "When I go into labor. I want all the drugs I can get. In fact, I'd like an epidural right now."

Zola continued without even listening to Min. "It's very important you think things over very carefully and then decide for yourself if you want to have an abortion."

"Abortion!" Min said. "Who said anything about having an abortion? I don't think I could do that."

"Well, of course you're going to have an abortion, Min," Zola said evenly.

"You just told me it was my decision," Min said. Her lower lip trembled. She felt about four years old, completely unprepared to handle anything as momentous as being pregnant.

"It is your decision," Zola said.

"You might not even be pregnant. Why don't we buy a pregnancy test kit?" Sally said.

Min, Zola, and Olivia looked at her, surprised. No one expected Sally to be the voice of reason.

"Sally's right, Min," Zola said. "We better First Response your ass."

(A New Low)

Clarence Terence looked on in complete disgust. Why did these girls insist on making everything so complicated? It was as though they had made a pact to keep him from getting his job done. He even tossed them a bone—his great-grandnephew Myles. And what did they do? Spit it out. Myles was almost as handsome as Clarence was, and he'd be almost as smart if he would just get over himself. But you'd have thought Myles was butt ugly by the way those girls treated him.

Clarence set up a felt-topped card table and folding chair on the corner and waited for the girls to walk by. He wrapped a purple beach towel around his head like a turban, put on M·A·C Russian Red lipstick, and gave himself a large black beauty mark near the corner of his mouth with an eyeliner.

How dare they second-guess him by going to that hag of a fortune-telling nutcase? He had never been so insulted in his life. Did Dorothy go for a second opinion after Glinda the Good Witch showed up? Did Cinderella check up on her fairy godmother behind her back? This was definitely a new low point.

Clarence checked his reflection in his compact. He looked like a bitchy transvestite cabaret singer. But of course he looked bitchy—he was feeling bitchy.

He looked at his watch. Ten seconds. Five. Three, two, one.

Zola, Olivia, Sally, and Min walked by. They stopped when they saw him.

"Lenny?" Sally said.

He was staring into a multicolored beach ball as if it were a crystal ball.

"Hello, my beautiful young ladies," he said in a fake thick Russian accent. He was trying to sound like Rose Schwartz. "I am ze great Madame Nemgrimeva and I can tell you your future for a good price." Actually his Russian accent wasn't half bad. He had studied acting briefly at the Lee Strasberg Institute in New York in the early sixties.

"What are you doing?" Zola asked. "You look ridiculous."

Clarence couldn't believe he had to sit there dressed in an absurd outfit to get their attention. And they only looked mildly surprised. Maybe all that stuff on the news lately is really true, he thought. It *is* getting tougher and tougher to shock today's teens.

"So. I see you don't trust me?" Clarence said.

The girls looked at him guiltily.

He shuffled a deck of playing cards on the little table. "Pick a card, any card," he said to Min. She picked one and then he had her pick three more. He laid the cards on the table. "Let's see," he said. "The ace of spades. The seven of hearts. The queen of clubs. And the eight of clubs."

Sally was starting to feel dizzy again.

"What can you tell from that?" Min asked.

"Nothing," Clarence said, laughing.

Zola was annoyed. "We really don't have time for these little games," she said.

"Well, *excuse* me," Clarence said, hurt. "Listen, children learn by playing games. If you don't trust me, at least trust Mr. Rogers. You could learn a thing or two from a wise man such as him. But Rose Schwartz? You cheat on me with Rose Schwartz? That's just plain insulting."

"We didn't mean to insult you," Sally said. She felt like crying. Life was so confusing.

"We don't know what to do," Olivia said, as if that explained everything. And it did, pretty much.

"Stay in school," Clarence said. "Tomorrow is another day. And it's a school day, thank God." He sounded like an overworked stay-at-home mom who was at her wits' end.

"I think I'm pregnant," Min whispered to Clarence.

Clarence put his hand on her stomach. "The only thing you're carrying is a couple of matzo balls from dinner last night," he said.

Min wasn't convinced. The only thing she would believe right now was a negative E.P.T.

"Is anything going to change?" Sally asked hopelessly.

"Things will change if you look for signs and follow them," he said. Clarence handed her a Magic 8 Ball.

Sally took the plastic ball and shook it. Then she peered into the little round window, waiting for her answer to appear in the blue liquid.

"'Try again later,'" she read.

9

(Ozzy and Harriet)

Min let herself into the house and was just about to start up the stairs to her room when she heard her father's voice and then Tobias's voice in the dining room. For a moment she froze. She was nervous someone would see the pregnancy test kit in her pocketbook, even though it was in a brown paper bag and buried deep at the bottom.

Was it her imagination or did she just hear her father say the word *pregnant?*

"Yes, pregnant," she heard Tobias say. "I'm sorry I wasn't more careful."

Min was horrified. Lenny was wrong! But how could they possibly know? Could her parents somehow tell she was pregnant? Did Tobias tell them what they had done last night? Her mind was working a million miles a minute, trying to figure out how any of them could know.

"I really didn't expect this from someone in your household," a strange woman said. Who was she? Min couldn't recognize the voice. "After all, you're a rabbi. A rabbi!" the woman said.

"That's true, Mrs. Greenspan, but these things do happen. It's an act of God. An act of nature. I'm sure Min and Tobias are very, very sorry about this."

Min's heart was beating so loud, she could hardly hear their conversation. Mrs. Greenspan was their next-door neighbor. How on earth could *she* know Min was pregnant? Min searched for an answer. The only thing she could think of was the café. Mrs. Greenspan must have been there and overheard. That would be just Min's luck. What a bitch! She had come running back to tell Min's father. Min burst into frightened tears.

"I just don't see how you could let him run loose like that. It really is a disgrace," Mrs. Greenspan said. "They're not even the same breed."

"Well, at least they're both Jewish," Min's father said, laughing.

Min couldn't believe her father could laugh at a time like this. But it was a good sign. Maybe he would be understanding.

"How can you make a joke, Rabbi Weinstock?" Mrs. Greenspan said. "It's disgusting and entirely irresponsible."

"It was pretty irresponsible behavior, Tobias," Min's father said. It sounded like he was stifling a laugh. Min couldn't believe it. What was wrong with him?

"Have you put any thought into who will bear the expense of all this?"

"Of course I'll pay for everything, ma'am," Tobias said. "I can't wait to see what they look like." *They?* How did he know she was having twins? Tobias sounded so excited, Min felt guilty for even thinking of aborting.

"What do you expect to do with the little rugrats?" Rabbi Weinstock asked cheerfully.

Rugrats! Min thought, horrified. And what did he mean, *do* with them? That was some way to talk about your future grandchildren.

"I don't know yet," Tobias said. "Sell them or give them away."

Min couldn't take it anymore. She stormed into the dining room.

"Min," her father said. "Are you all right? You look sick."

"Guess who's going to be a daddy!" Tobias said. He was positively glowing.

Min looked at him in complete disbelief.

"Ozzy! The little devil. Who knew he had it in him? He got that little shih tzu next door pregnant. And she's about twice his size. Mrs. Greenspan caught them at it again last week and the vet confirmed it this morning. What a way to start the day, eh, boy?"

Ozzy lay on his back under the dining-room table. Min could almost imagine him smoking a cigar.

9½

(Magic Wand)

Min's head was spinning. First babies, now puppies. She didn't know what to think. But she had to go through with it. Locking the bathroom door, she ripped open the box containing the pregnancy test kit. There were instructions, a white plastic thing that looked like a small magic wand, and a small plastic cup. At first Min couldn't understand the instructions, but then she figured out she was reading them in Spanish.

She turned over the instruction sheet and read it more carefully than she had ever read anything in her life. If she had paid that much attention to her chemistry textbook, she might have done better than a C average.

She had to pee in the cup and then stick the magic wand in the pee, but not too far into the pee, only up to the tip. Then she had to lay the wand on a flat surface for three minutes. If a blue cross appeared in the tiny window on the tip of the wand, that meant she had done the test correctly. If a red line appeared beneath it, it meant she was pregnant.

She sat down on the toilet and carefully peed into the cup. "Dear God," she whispered. "If I'm not pregnant, I promise to do one good deed a day for the rest of my life." She placed the cup on the tile floor, but before she even had a chance to complete the test, she noticed one very important thing. She had her period. There was definitely no denying it. She should have bought Tampax and Midol at the drugstore, not an E.P.T. kit. The only one who was pregnant was Harriet, Mrs. Greenspan's two-year-old shih tzu.

Min let out the biggest sigh of relief of her entire life. Then she laughed giddily. She felt like she'd been holding her breath all morning and her brain hadn't gotten enough oxygen. Was this what people meant when they said, "Don't do drugs; get high on life"? Min giggled again. Probably not.

She dumped the pee into the toilet and put the cup, the wand, the instructions, and the ripped open box back into the brown paper bag. Then she shoved it all deep inside her pocketbook. She would have to smuggle out the bag and dispose of it elsewhere. It wasn't exactly the kind of thing you tossed in your own wastepaper basket where your mother would find it.

She went into her room and collapsed onto her bed.

This whole day had been exhausting. And expensive. Five dollars for a psychic who had confused her with a dog, four dollars for coffee, and eleven dollars for a pregnancy test kit she didn't even need.

She had to call Zola, Olivia, and Sally and tell them the good news.

She picked up the phone and started to dial Zola's number, but just then Tobias walked into her room without knocking, so she hung up. He put Ozzy down on the bed, and Ozzy sniffed all around and then ran over to Min's head and started licking her left ear. Tobias sat on the side of her bed and put his hand on her stomach.

Min sat up. "Tobias, you know you're not allowed in here."

"Your dad went out for a while. You didn't even congratulate Ozzy on being a daddy to be. And I wuff you. We wuff our Min-Min."

Min-Min was starting to hate it when Tob-Tob talked puppy talk. It was really getting old.

"Can't you ever be serious?" she asked.

"Yes, I can be serious," Tobias said in a serious voice. "Why don't I go out and put on a suit and tie and come back in when I'm dressed more appropriately for this conversation?"

Min remembered her pregnancy promise to God. "Do

you ever think about doing something for someone else? You know, like a good deed?"

"Like what?" Tobias asked. He took the little white bonnet off a stuffed bunny rabbit Min had on the chair next to her bed and tied it on Ozzy's head. "Ozzy rabbit," he said. The white ruffle covered Ozzy's eyes, and he scratched at it, trying to get it off.

"Like feeding homeless people or something," Min said.

Tobias stood up. "You know, Min, you're sort of being a drip lately, you know that?" He left with Ozzy, still wearing the bonnet.

Min grabbed the stuffed rabbit and shoved it under her shirt. She went to the full-length mirror on the closet door and looked at herself with a big stomach.

⑩

(Mr. Creepies)

That night Zola had horrible dreams about Claudia Choney. She dreamed she was sitting in a strange movie theater, watching Claudia and Evan kissing on the big screen. When she tried to leave the theater, she found that the bottoms of her shoes were stuck to the floor with chewing gum.

She woke up wanting to kill Claudia even more. She wanted to rip the tongue stud right out of her mouth with her tongue still attached.

Her alarm went off. School. Shit. She went into her little brother Nathaniel's room and picked out pants, a blue-and-red-striped T-shirt, tighty whiteys, and a pair of socks and put them on the foot of his bed. "It's uppy time," she whispered into his ear. "Brush your teeth and drink a whole glass of milk." Even though he was eight, he still liked words like *uppy time.*

"Mommy," he said, and put his arms out toward her. He was still asleep.

Zola looked over at the framed picture of her mother that Nathaniel kept on his little-kid desk. In the picture her mother was standing on the back porch with a glass of water in her hand, holding it toward the camera and smiling cheesily as if to say, "Try it. It's the best damn water I ever tasted!" The picture was taken six years ago, and her hair was styled almost exactly the same as Zola's was now. She must have stopped cutting it shortly after the picture was taken because when she died, it was past her shoulders.

Zola wondered if Nathaniel really remembered their mother or if he only thought he did because of the photograph. Was he dreaming about her? Zola wished she could crawl inside his dream with him so they could all be together again.

She shook him gently and gave him a hug. "Hi, Zo," Nathaniel said with a big smile. "I get to feed a whole mouse to Mr. Creepies today in science period."

Zola wondered what it would be like to feel genuinely excited about feeding a mouse to a snake named Mr. Creepies. Or even to look forward to going to school at all.

"All right. Let's get the show on the road," she said.

They both had very big days ahead of them. Nathaniel had his snake. And Zola had hers.

⑪

(**Help Each Other**)

As soon as they got to homeroom the voice of Mr. Seidman, the principal, came over the PA system ominously announcing that there was an assembly.

And then there were three announcements:

"Congratulations to Claudia Choney and Evan Fell, queen and king of the prom." (Everyone in the room turned to stare at Zola.)

"The names of the valedictorian and salutatorian will be announced tomorrow." (Again everyone turned to stare at Zola because they knew the valedictorian was probably going to be Claudia.)

"And would Zola Mitchell please come to the principal's office ASAP?" (Needless to say, everyone just kept staring.)

Zola slithered out of her attached desk chair, unfazed. She had a feeling that this had something to do with a certain sign she had been forced to paint congratulating

Claudia and Evan on being prom queen and king, due to having attempted to flush the first one down the toilet. She had painted *Clawdia* on the sign instead of *Claudia,* an honest mistake that anyone could have made, and hung it in the cafeteria.

She walked calmly out of homeroom, with the grace and majesty of Anne Boleyn, one of Henry VIII's beheaded wives. At least there was a good side to all this. She might get to miss the assembly. At the last one they had to suffer through four hours of flamenco dancing, and the one before that they had to listen to that old Irish guy who wrote *Angela's Ashes* drone on for practically the whole day. And nothing was worse than the one before that, a "play" called *No Means No Way* about date rape with the worst acting you'd ever seen in your life. But at least for those assemblies she had been sitting next to Evan, holding hands with him discreetly.

Zola sat in Mr. Seidman's office, where she had been told to wait. It was fine with her. What else did she have to do? Why did they even bother to make seniors show up at school between prom and graduation?

She stretched out her long legs and rested her feet on Mr. Seidman's desk and accidentally knocked over his stupid "Don't Let the Turkeys Get You Down" mug of coffee. She sat up straight and looked for something to clean up the mess, but there wasn't anything around except Mr.

Seidman's ugly black cardigan. She grabbed it from the back of his chair and used the sleeve to wipe up the spill.

Then she noticed what she was cleaning up. Three manila folders. One marked "Claudia Choney," one marked "Olivia Dawes," and one marked "William Buchanan." She opened Claudia's file and found a green-and-white-striped computer printout of her transcript. Zola scanned it quickly. In four years of high school Claudia had earned grades all in the high nineties. Her lowest grade was one ninety-six in music. Her tongue stud must have gotten in the way of her playing the recorder. Zola was surprised. She had thought Claudia had been too busy stealing people's boyfriends to have found much time to study. Obviously she was wrong.

Zola's heart was pounding. She opened Olivia's file and then Bill's. From what she could tell, Claudia was ranked first, Bill was ranked second, and Olivia was ranked third. Zola was impressed with Olivia's records. She knew her friend was smart, but she hadn't realized how smart. Olivia had always been sort of hush-hush about her grades because she thought it was uncool to be *that* smart.

Zola was thinking as fast as she could. Olivia was in third place because she had slacked off a little in English her senior year. With an eighty-seven, it was her worst sub-ject. She must have been too busy studying biology with Bill in the lab closet to read her English books. Not to mention all that time she spent getting her hair straightened. But it didn't seem fair to Zola that Olivia should lose out on being salutatorian just because she had naturally curly hair.

She certainly couldn't let Claudia steal her boyfriend, win prom queen, *and* get valedictorian. That would be beyond wrong.

If she wanted to change anything, she'd have to get into the computer, change the grades, and then print out new transcripts and put them in Mr. Seidman's folders. But if Claudia didn't make valedictorian, she was sure to request an official review of the records. Zola would have to think of everything. She knew they disregarded the one best grade and the one worst grade of each student like they did in the Miss America pageant. But maybe there were some other things that she was unaware of. For instance, if it was all based on grades, why were they waiting until tomorrow to announce the names? She was pretty sure they weren't going to have a bathing suit or talent category, but in this school anything was possible.

The bell rang for second period, and there was still no sign of Mr. Seidman. Zola had to act fast.

She turned on his computer. *Password* flashed on the screen. She thought for a moment and then typed in the word *turkey. Password error* flashed on the screen. She tried a few more words. *Seidman. La Follette. Melanie.*

That was his daughter's name. Melanie was such a stoner, she'd had to repeat tenth grade. It was one of La Follette's many scandals. *Melanie* didn't work. This was useless.

Then Zola noticed a small yellow Post-it on the edge of the screen. It said, *New password: knowledge.* What a dork! She typed in *knowledge,* and a list of files came on the screen.

Within minutes Zola had raised several of Olivia's grades, lowered a few of Claudia's, printed up new transcripts, and stuck them in the folders. She couldn't believe it could be that easy. Olivia was now ranked one, Bill was ranked two, and Claudia was a sad and lonely number three. Sorry, bitch. Better luck next time.

Zola's heart was racing so fast in her chest, she thought she was going to shoot straight into the air. She shut down the computer and shoved the old transcripts into her book bag just as Mr. Seidman walked into the room.

Mr. Seidman didn't know what to make of Zola. Ever since the Columbine incident you couldn't be too careful. Zola was supposed to have painted a sign saying, Congratulations, Claudia and Evan, Our Prom Queen and King! But of course she hadn't followed directions.

"What is the meaning of your little banner?" Mr. Seidman said. The banner wasn't too awful—it could have been far, far worse—he just didn't understand why she'd done it.

Zola played innocent. "I don't know what you're talking about," she said. They couldn't very well expel her for painting a *w* instead of a *u*. She would just pretend she didn't know she had spelled Claudia's name wrong.

"Follow me," Mr. Seidman said.

She followed him along a long corridor, down a flight of stairs, and down another long corridor into the cafeteria. He pointed to the banner. But it wasn't even the banner she had painted. It was a totally new banner. It said, Help Each Other, in huge rainbow letters. It was very corny, and definitely not Zola's work.

"That's a nice sentiment, Zolar, but it's not what you were asked to do."

"I didn't paint that," Zola protested. "I don't even know what it means." Help each other. Help each other. That sounded like something Lenny would say. And he had told them to follow the signs. "Things will change if you look for signs and follow them," he had said. Here was a sign. *Help each other.* So that's what they were supposed to do? Well, she'd already done that.

Upstairs in the art room, Clarence Terence stood at the sink, rinsing out his brushes. He felt much better. Painting could be so therapeutic.

(Self-Defense)

The assembly looked like it was going to be the worst one ever. It was a demonstration on self-defense. A man was dressed from head to toe in an enormous orange padded outfit, like a gigantic round Oompa Loompa or a huge version of a South Park character. A tiny woman wearing a Madonna-style headset screamed at him and punched, kicked, and head butted him. At first it was mildly amusing, especially when she accidentally yelled a filthy word at him before attacking.

Sally was quietly minding her own business, writing in her diary on her lap, when the little woman walked down the aisle, grabbed her hand, and dragged her toward the stage. Sally tried to pull away, but the woman wouldn't take no for an answer. She pulled Sally up onstage, and Sally scanned the auditorium, looking for Min, Olivia, or Zola, but she couldn't see them anywhere.

"All right, now what do you do if you see this man

following you and you start to feel suspicious?" the woman asked Sally.

Sally didn't know what she would do if she saw a man dressed like a balloon in the Thanksgiving Day parade following her. The man waddled over to her and tried to grab her arm.

"Scream *no*," the woman instructed.

Sally whispered the word *no*.

"Scream it," the woman yelled.

"Hey, Sally," a boy from the audience shouted. It sounded like moronic Mike Cantona. "He's wearing more padding than you are!"

Everyone in the whole auditorium laughed.

"Look, it's a Victoria's Secret model," someone else shouted.

"Let's see that bra again, Sally!"

Sally stood helplessly on the stage as it slowly began to dawn on her that the entire school had seen her talking about her bra on TV. Then as if a supernatural force had entered her body, she took a deep breath and screamed the word *no*. The sound came from somewhere deep, deep inside of her and echoed in her ears. It was exhilarating to scream like that. She put her head down and like a bull in Barcelona, Spain, she charged at the orange padded man.

(12)

(Favorite Uncle)

"Not too full!" Clarence shouted at his great-grandnephew, Myles, who was filling saltshakers. Clarence was dressed like a chef, complete with black clogs, black-and-white-checked pants, a big long apron, and a chef's hat. Myles hadn't even recognized him.

They were preparing for the lunch rush, and Clarence wanted to make sure his great-grandnephew didn't get fired on his second day of work. Summer had barely started, but what with the college and the high school both letting out this week, there were absolutely no more jobs to be had in Madison.

Clarence had gone to a lot of trouble to get Myles the job in the first place. He'd forged a letter to an adorable visiting French student who was going to waitress there, pretending to be the manager and telling her that the café was making a gradual shift toward becoming a beer-only pub. They were going to change its name to "Behemoth" and specialize in darts and World Cup soccer events and have a Thursday night "piss-in" where beer was free until somebody went to the bathroom or left. She might want to rethink her job choice, he wrote. The French girl never showed up, and the manager was frantic. That very day Myles turned up looking for work, and the manager gave him the job.

But Myles was oblivious. All he did all day was look at himself in the mirror and practice playing his saxophone. And he was good, too. If Clarence could just keep him out of trouble and get him to go to college in Madison for one semester, he would meet five guys, start a band with them, and later become one of the most famous sax players in the world.

Or he could spend the rest of the day smoking pot in the pantry at Bohème with Alexander, the Israeli dishwasher, get fired, leave Madison in a huff, and wind up playing outside shitty tourist bars in Mexico for a few pesos for beer.

What Myles needed was incentive.

"Oh, man!" Myles said, spilling salt all over the counter. "Damn!" he cried as the salt poured onto the floor and all over his boots.

Myles was never going to get anywhere with his music if he was that clumsy. "Get a broom, Myles," Clarence said.

Myles looked up. "Uncle Clarence?" he said, surprised.

All this time he'd thought he was working alongside the regular head chef, Spen, an aloof Hungarian who chain-smoked Kools. He didn't know his uncle Clarence could cook.

"Yes, it's me," Clarence said. "I am not a hallucination. You're not that high."

"Just as smooth as ever," Myles said approvingly. He spread his arms wide to give Clarence a big bear hug. "You know you've always been my favorite uncle."

Clarence tried to looked stern and maintain manly aloofness, but he was secretly pleased as punch.

"All right, favorite great-grandnephew," he said. "For that compliment you get a special treat. There's something I'd like you to do right now."

"But my shift's not over yet," Myles protested.

"Don't worry, I'll cover for you," Clarence assured him.

(13)

(Tuesday Tuna)

Zola, Olivia, Min, and Sally sat at their usual table in the cafeteria, eating Tuesday tuna. They were each feeling a little bit out of it. Zola was immensely pleased with herself for rigging the valedictorian pick, but she didn't want to tell the others what she had done. She didn't know how Olivia would feel about being picked valedictorian through dishonest means, and you could never tell when Min would get all self-righteous and politically correct. Her father was a rabbi, after all, and she didn't believe in cheating. It did feel weird, though, keeping it from her friends.

Sally was more dazed and confused than usual after the assembly from hell. She had actually wanted to go home, but when she went to the nurse's office, the nurse told her it was no wonder she had fainted. She was probably on some kind of starvation diet like most of the other girls in her class. The nurse told her to go to the cafeteria and get some lunch.

Olivia was deep in fantasyland about Holden and how

she was going to meet up with him again. She could just imagine having sex with him in the laundry room of his dorm, on top of one of the washing machines while it was on the spin cycle. College dorms were so sexy, with all those boys walking around looking like they had just stepped off the pages of *GQ*.

And Min was completely exhausted by her attempts to break up with Tobias. If only she could say, "I think we should spend some time apart." That way she could gain some distance, have time to think, take hot baths, make peace with her decision. But Tobias and Ozzy were still living in her basement. Just that morning Min had come down to the kitchen to find Tobias and her father in the middle of a crossword puzzle bonanza. Her father was hopping up and down on one foot, holding a box of Special K and shouting "Cosmic? No? *S? S?*—yes, yes. I've got it—*stellar!*"

"Rabbi Weinstock, you are the king!" Tobias had cried with his mouth full of bagel, eagerly filling in the letters. Ozzy was sitting in a chair, eating turkey bacon from a plate at the table, a cloth napkin tied around his neck to keep his fur clean. They didn't even notice Min come in. She was like a stranger in her own house. For once she was actually glad to go to school.

The girls looked up at the "Help Each Other" sign over their heads.

"Definitely Lenny," they agreed.

"I think it's a message for us," Zola said. "We can't just work on changing our own futures individually. We have to work as a team and . . ." She pointed up at the sign.

". . . help each other," they all said in unison, cracking up.

"I think we should focus on one of us at a time," Zola said, "and I suggest we start with the easiest—Min breaking up with Tobias. I mean, how hard can it really be?"

Min nodded, trying to feel determined. "All right," she agreed. "I'll do it."

"And whose future would you say is the hardest to change?" Sally asked.

"Well, yours, obviously," Zola answered. "Getting you laid is not exactly going to be easy." Zola laughed and Olivia cackled along with her.

"Oh, come on, Sal, you walked right into that one," Olivia said.

"So I'm first," Min said dubiously. "Fine."

Just then the impossibly hot waiter from the café they'd gone to the day before walked across the cafeteria toward them, carrying a tray.

"Who's that guy?" Min asked.

"It's that waiter guy," Olivia said. "The cute one you wouldn't let me talk to yesterday."

"What's he doing here?" Zola said, frowning.

"Lenny," Sally whispered. But the other girls didn't hear her. They were too busy drooling.

(New in Town)

Myles surveyed the cafeteria. He was still a little baked from his morning joint, and he had a serious craving for rice pudding. The last thing he wanted to eat was tuna. But he had promised Uncle Clarence. Besides, those four girls were cute, especially the dimply dark-haired one. He wanted to rest his hands on her hips and slow dance to Santana with her.

"Hey," Zola said, loudly enough to get his attention.

"Hey," Myles said back. He knew he'd never get it on with that one. She had too much attitude.

"Are you lost or something?" Zola asked.

"Uh, I don't think so. It's lunchtime and this looks like the cafeteria," Myles said with a shit-eating grin that would win your grandmother over in a heartbeat.

"What tipped you off?" Zola asked, raising her eyebrows cockily.

Myles laughed. He pointed to the banner. "I guess you're just trying to *help* me," he said.

"Yeah, we're really friendly in these here parts," Olivia said, flirting.

"That's great," Myles said. "I'm new in town."

"Do you always eat in high school cafeterias?" Min asked.

"Well, it's a good way to get to know the natives," Myles said.

The girls invited him to sit down with them and then introduced themselves.

"I'm Myles Davies," he said. He already sounded famous. Sally couldn't stop staring at his hands. They were lovely, lovely hands.

"Min," Myles said, turning to Min. "That's a cool name."

"It's short for Wilamina," Min said.

The other girls were surprised. Min hardly ever told anyone her real name. Myles looked deeply into Min's shining brown eyes. Min blushed.

"Myles Davies is a really cool name," she said.

"Hey, Myles," Zola interrupted them. "They're going to stop serving pretty soon. If you want lunch, you better go up there before Hair Net Betty closes the joint."

"Thanks," Myles said, standing up. "Does anybody want anything?" Zola shot Olivia a look. He was considerate. Polite. Well trained. What a refreshing change.

"I'll go with you," Min said.

Olivia kicked Zola under the table as Min and Myles

walked over to the food service area together. This was so exciting!

"I don't know why we didn't think about it before," Zola said.

"What?" Sally asked, suddenly paying attention now that Myles had left.

"What's the easiest way to break up with someone?" Zola prodded.

"Start going out with someone else!" Olivia trumpeted.

"Are we ready to *help each other*?" Zola asked, pointing at Min and Myles.

"Yes, definitely," Olivia agreed. "We've got to make sure this happens."

Sally looked at Myles and Min in line for food. Myles dipped his finger in a little bowl of Jell-O pudding and dabbed it on the tip of Min's nose. Min tried to lick it off, giggling and ruffling her feathers.

It didn't seem like there was going to be very much for them to do.

(Frankenstein)

Olivia looked at her watch. There were only twenty-five minutes left in seventh period. She was supposed to be in study hall, finishing her English extra-credit paper. But she just couldn't face writing it, even though her grade could be the difference between valedictorian, salutatorian, or nothing. Now she was in front of the lab closet, waiting for Bill. Normally she looked forward to their little rendezvous. It was a welcome break in the day. But all Olivia could do was think about Holden. She was sort of hoping Bill wouldn't even show up.

It was crazy. She and Holden had only talked for five minutes on Sunday at the bookstore, but she had felt an instant spark. Still, she had no idea how he felt about her. He hadn't called or e-mailed, and she certainly couldn't call him. She had literally memorized the book *The Rules* in its entirety over Christmas break and always followed its advice to the letter.

Olivia couldn't get Holden out of her mind. Every single period that day she had asked to be excused to use the bathroom so she could call her machine from the pay phone. But nothing. No new messages.

What was she going to do? She just had to see him again.

"Hey," Bill said, strolling into the lab. "Sorry I'm late." He walked over to her and put his arms around her. "How about we get started on our little research project since we don't have much time?" he said. "I'll be the control group."

Bill usually got a laugh out of Olivia from this sort of thing, but today she looked at him like he was some kind of untouchable.

He kissed her and she kissed him back. He was wearing his Space Camp T-shirt, which Olivia had always found incredibly sexy even if it was a little immature. "Welcome to my la-*bor*-atory," Bill said, laughing like Frankenstein. He opened the door to the storage closet and she followed him in.

She unzipped Bill's corduroys, wishing they were Holden's corduroys. She rested her head on Bill's shoulder, wishing it were Holden's shoulder. Holden, Holden, she thought. The best thing about Holden was the way he smelled. Like shaving cream. Plus he wore sandals. Olivia loved guys in sandals. She looked down at Bill's faded black Converse sneakers with broken laces and worn-down heels. And then she did something she'd never done before. She left.

She just had to try her machine one more time before eighth period.

(The Plan)

When Olivia got to the pay phones out in the hall, she found Zola, Sally, and Min standing in front of them, talking excitedly.

Myles Davies had asked Min out. Min had said yes, but she hadn't told him about Tobias. Myles wanted to go out after school, but Min was supposed to meet Tobias at the mall to help him buy an interview suit and tie at You're the Man. And then they were supposed to have dinner.

They all forgot about the calls they had been about to make—Olivia to her machine to see if Holden had called, Zola to her machine to see if Evan had called, and Sally to her mother to tell her she had fainted in assembly and could she come pick her up. Now they were completely focused on getting Min out of her date with Tobias or, as Zola sometimes liked to call him, Tub-ass.

"I just tried calling my house and he already left. He could be anywhere on the whole college campus. There's no way to reach him," Min said dejectedly. "I'll just have to tell Myles I can't go."

"It's better if you don't see him today, anyway," Olivia said. "You shouldn't be available on such short notice. It's good to tell him you're busy." She was getting really into her *Rules*-speak. "But don't tell him you have another date. Don't tell him *what* you're doing. Be mysterious—"

"Will you stop with that crap?" Zola said, interrupting Olivia as fast as she could. "Min, forget about Tub-ass. You have to go out with Myles. You already said yes, didn't you?"

Min blushed. "Yes," she said. "He was so sweet about it, the word *yes* just came out of my mouth. Can you believe it?" Min was so excited, she was practically squeaking.

"Then just stand Tub-ass up," Zola said, as if it was the easiest thing in the world. "Later you can tell him you were sick. Or you can tell him one of us got sick. Tell him you had to take Sally to the hospital because she got so upset that everyone saw her talking about her bra on television."

"Don't tell him that," Sally said, glaring at Zola.

"I can't stand him up, Zola," Min said. "And don't call him Tub-ass."

Zola groaned, exasperated. Did Min want to change her future or didn't she? Zola felt like she was the only one following through.

"*Why* can't you stand him up?" Zola asked angrily.

"*Why* can't you chill out?" Min asked, mimicking Zola's tone of voice. "I can't let Tobias just stand there waiting for me. And he really needs help picking out clothes. I don't want him going for that Regis Philbin solid color-tie look. And I have to be there to smuggle Ozzy in, in my book bag, or the security guard won't let him in."

"Fine," Zola said. "Then I guess we'll just have to cover for you. I'll take him to You're the Man if I have to. I'll be there at four o'clock and I'll tell him you had to stay after school."

Min thought this through for a minute. She thought of Myles with his adorable short dreadlocks and his cool red jeans. She hadn't been on a date with anyone but Tobias in almost two years.

"Okay," she said, half guiltily and half excitedly.

⬤ 15

(You're the Man)

As soon as Zola got to the You're the Man store she saw Tub-ass standing there looking more like a lost puppy than Ozzy, who was happily enjoying the coolness of the mall floor.

"Hey," she said.

"Hey," he said.

They were off to a great start.

"Uh," he said after a couple of seconds. "Do you happen to know where Min is?"

"She wanted me to tell you she couldn't make it. She got in trouble for passing notes in English and she had to stay after school."

He took off his blue fisherman's hat and ran his fingers through his hair. Actually his hair was kind of nice, sort of sandy and fluffy soft. "We were supposed to buy me a suit," Tobias said.

"Oh, you were?" Zola said. "You know, if you want, I

81

could help you. I could really see you in a dark three-button Armani."

Tobias cocked his head like a squirrel in the park. "All right, Zo," he said cautiously. "If you really want to." He couldn't figure out why Zola, of all people, was being nice to him.

"Cool," Zola said.

They walked into the store and a dorky short guy came barreling over. "What can I do for you, sir?" he asked.

"Do you have any Armani?" Tobias asked.

Zola practically burst out laughing. It was sort of sweet, really. All you had to do to get along with a man was compliment the hell out of him. They followed the salesman over to the suit department. "Armani," the man said, indicating a small rack of suits. "You have excellent taste, sir." Tobias looked at all the price tags and frowned.

"Perhaps you'd like to see something in the You're the Man's own line of suits?"

Zola jumped in. "Yes, we would," she said. This was actually her particular specialty—finding cool, wearable shit in discount stores. You had to have a good eye. Tub-ass was lucky she came. "Tobias, I think you'll look great in gray or navy."

While Tobias was in the dressing room, trying on three different suits, Zola looked around a little. She found her way to a table of boxer shorts with different things printed on them. There were pairs with golf balls, American flags, mermaids, sharks, lawn mowers, motor-cycles, guitars. Zola was suddenly overcome with sad-ness. The guitar pair would be perfect for Evan. If only she could buy them for him and surprise him. He looked so hot in boxers, even though he usually wore briefs. God, she missed him.

"I miss him," Zola whispered to Ozzy, who was being very well behaved in her book bag. Ozzy looked up at her as if he understood. "You know, you're pretty cute," she said to him, and petted the top of his head with her finger. "I can see why all the girls go for you." It was sort of com-forting to have Ozzy to talk to. She was beginning to see why Min liked the little guy so much.

Well, at least she had Lenny. She grabbed the motor-cycle boxers in a size medium and took them up to the cash register. Then she went back to find Tobias.

He looked kind of amazing in the blue suit. What a dif-ference from his usual faded jeans and one of the four UW T-shirts he always wore.

"What did you buy?" Tobias asked her.

"Pair of boxers."

"For your boyfriend?" he asked, kind of smiling.

"I don't have a boyfriend. Anymore," Zola said.

"Why? What happened?" Tobias looked like he really

wanted to know. Like he was genuinely interested.

Before she knew it, while they chose a shirt, looked at belts, and selected a pack of black Gold Toe socks, Zola had poured out her heart to Tub-ass. But she wasn't thinking of him as Tub-ass so much anymore.

"Zola, that dude Evan is crazy to let you go. It's totally his loss. I would bet the price of those Armani suits that he'll come crawling back. Any guy would," Tobias said.

"You really think so?"

"Evan doesn't know what he's doing. I've seen that girl Claudia. She gives new meaning to the word *hoochie.* She probably has diseases. Forget about it—you are *so* much better looking than she is," Tobias said.

Zola did something she'd never done in her entire life. She blushed. She could feel her face get hot, and she looked at herself in a mirror near the suspenders. She was beet red. And she did look pretty. She'd had no idea that Tobias was so easy to talk to.

"Come on," she said, "let's get you a tie."

By the time she was done with Tobias, he didn't look anything like Regis Philbin. He looked more like a combination of Vince Vaughn and that Australian guy in *10 Things I Hate About You.*

They picked out two ties. One conservative tie with a

blue-and-yellow pattern and a purple one with little white puppies on it. "Do you think Min will like me in this?" he asked, holding it up to his chest.

Tobias looked so in love, talking about Min. Zola felt guilty knowing Min was right at that moment getting ready for a date with another man. But she shook herself out of it. They had their futures to think about.

"Oh, Min would *love* you in that," she said.

(Destiny)

Clarence Terence deserved a massage. Whenever he was in Madison, he always went to Mario, who had the best pair of hands on the planet. Clarence lay face-down on the wooden Oakworks massage table and stared down at Mario's white Aerosole sneakers through the headrest. If people were going to be staring at his feet all day, he thought, he would be sure to wear some cooler sneakers. But Mario was a cool guy. His dream was to be the official massage therapist for the Green Bay Packers. That hadn't happened. Yet. Clarence knew that massaging the Packers was definitely in Mario's cards. All he had to do was go to the local dinner theater production of *Guys & Dolls* that night. The wife of one of the Packers would be there. She was going to fall on the stairs and throw her back out and Mario was going to be there to fix her up. Tomorrow Mario would get a call from the manager, and he'd be moving to Green Bay by the end of the week.

"You're tense, Clarence," Mario said.

Clarence groaned. "I feel better already."

"I haven't even done anything yet," Mario said.

Just the feel of the massage lotion on his back relaxed him. There was nothing in the world like a massage. He would have to treat Zola, Min, Olivia, and Sally to a massage from Mario.

Damn it. There he was, thinking about them again. He had promised himself he wouldn't think about the girls at all. It was his time off. He had been thinking about them nonstop. He was really beginning to become obsessive about the whole thing. Watching them and planning and scheming. He was acting the way they did when they liked a new boy. Like an idiot.

He had to stop. This was only a gig. He was trying to get to the next karmic level, but if it didn't work out this time, he would just have to live with it and try again with the next generation.

But he was starting to doubt himself. And now he had made things even more complicated by bringing his great-grandnephew into the mix. The important thing was to always act in the interest of the highest-possible good. But Clarence wondered if he had really done that. Manipulating a situation like he had done with Myles and Min was asking for trouble.

Still, it was a little late to have second thoughts. Now all he could do was worry.

"All right, we're done," Mario said.

Clarence looked at his watch. The hour had seemed like five minutes. He had been so up in his head, he hadn't even felt the massage. Here he was always telling people to be in the moment and he had been a million miles away.

"Mario," Clarence said. "I have a ticket for *Guys & Dolls* tonight over at the dinner theater and I'd like you to have it."

"Oh, no thanks," Mario said. "I hate musicals."

"I *really* think you should go," Clarence said, getting annoyed. Why did he have to spell everything out for everybody? He didn't want to get into the whole fairy god-mother thing with Mario while he was lying naked on a massage table. Mario might get the wrong idea.

"Why?"

"I just have a feeling," Clarence said. He pressed the ticket into his hand. "I know if you go, you'll thank me. You'll see."

Mario took the ticket and shrugged. "Okay, thanks."

Clarence wasn't sure if Mario would go, but there was really nothing he could do about it. You could lead a horse to water, but you couldn't make him drink.

He had planned on taking the rest of the day off, but he was curious to see how things were going with Min and Myles. Even he could only manipulate so much. The rest was either *bashert*—Yiddish for destiny—or it wasn't.

(17)
(Jonathon)

Min had never tasted anything as good as this pizza. You'd think she was eating pizza for the very first time. She savored each and every bite, gazing into Myles's gorgeous brown eyes. And it felt so nice to not have to share little bits of her crust and cheese with a dog.

Myles had ordered them both a root beer, which was very cute of him. They took a sip at exactly the same time. She watched Myles chew on his ice. Min was so happy, she felt like she could tell Myles anything.

"I have a boyfriend," she confessed. "But it's over."

"Oh?" Myles said, frowning with concern.

"We're breaking up," Min said, but her voice cracked a little. They just sat there for a few minutes with Min crumpling up her napkin and shredding it into tiny pieces.

"So I guess this thing with your boyfriend is pretty serious," Myles said. "How long have you been dating him?"

"A year and a half," Min said.

Myles thought for a minute. "Are you sure you want to do this? I mean, that's a long time. My longest relationship was only five weeks long. I can't even imagine what it would be like to stick with someone for a whole year and a half." He pulled his straw out of his root beer and inhaled on it, like a cigarette. Then he exhaled and leveled his gaze at Min, looking like the sexiest man ever born. "But I'd really like to find out."

Min was transfixed. She didn't even pause to think about what she was going to say next. "I'm ready to go out with someone else," she said.

"Well, I guess I can live with being the rebound guy, if I have to," Myles said, plunging his straw back into his root beer. "But I'd like to start off with something more than pizza. Let me take you out for a real date tonight."

Min remembered her first real date with Tobias, when they had gone to the pound to adopt Ozzy. What she had liked about Tobias at the time was that he seemed so old and mature. And now that they had been going out for so long, they knew each other well enough to communicate without talking. But what she liked about Myles, besides his amazing body, kissable lips, and delicious personality, was that he seemed so . . . exciting. It was fun being around someone she didn't know all that well. It felt really liberating.

"So what do you say?" Myles said. "We'll go back to

our places to change and then I'll pick you up for dinner tonight. Okay?"

"Well, I was sort of supposed to go out with Tobias—that's his name—to break up. I mean, I was going to do it tonight—totally end things."

"Okay," Myles said. "If that's what you want to do. Or . . ."

"What?" Min asked.

"You could end things with him tomorrow and *start* things with me tonight."

Min didn't know what to do. She needed help. "Would you excuse me?" she asked. "I just have to make a quick call." She went to the back of the pizza parlor and dialed Zola's cell phone number. Luckily she answered.

"It's me," Min said. "Are you still with Tobias?"

"Yes, I am," Zola said.

"Don't tell him it's me on the phone," Min said nervously.

"Okay, Jonathon," Zola said.

"Jonathon? Why Jonathon?" Min asked.

"I have no idea, Jonathon," Zola said. Min could hear Ozzy bark in the background. "Where are you?"

"I'm still with Myles," Min said. "And I was wondering if there was any way you could keep Tobias busy a little longer. Or actually a lot longer."

"So, I guess that means you're having a great time, Jonathon."

"Who's Jonathon?" Min heard Tobias say.

Min suddenly felt a pang of guilt. She wanted to tell Zola what a fantastic time she was having, but it didn't seem right to do it with Tobias standing right there. "Yeah, I'm having an okay time," Min said. "So, can you keep him occupied?"

"Of course. I'll figure something out," Zola said. "Olivia, Sally, and I are like the Charlie's Angels of dating."

"What does that mean?" Tobias said in the background.

"Just keep him away from my house," Min said.

"Don't worry about a thing, Jonathon," Zola said. "Just be sure to call me when you get home. I want to hear every detail. Promise me, Jonathon."

"I promise," Min said.

(Mission Impossible)

As soon as Zola got off the phone with Min she told Tobias she had to find a ladies' room and left him sitting on a bench in the mall with Ozzy's head sticking out of the You're the Man shopping bag, looking longingly at the mall fountain. Ozzy loved fountains of any kind.

In the ladies' room Zola called Olivia and asked if she could cover for her and baby-sit Tobias for a while.

"I was supposed to finish that English paper tonight," Olivia said.

Zola was bursting to tell Olivia about the grade switching she had done on the computer, but she kept her mouth shut. "Maybe you could work on the paper with Tobias," Zola suggested. "He is in college. Maybe he could help you."

Neither of them had any idea whether Tobias was a good student or not. But they had promised to help each other, and Zola knew Olivia would take her up on any chance to get out of the house.

"Come on," Zola said.

"All right," Olivia agreed. "Hey, Holden goes to the college, too. Maybe if I study in the college library with Tobias, I'll see Holden there!" All of a sudden she sounded excited.

"Great, Olivia," Zola said. "I love the way you're always thinking of others."

"Hey, what's the big deal? I'll be helping Min out, and I might get to see my gorgeous Holden at the same time," Olivia said.

"Right," Zola said, laughing. "Okay, I'm hanging up now. Call me on my cell phone in five minutes."

"Okay," Olivia said.

Zola went back to Tobias and Ozzy on their bench.

"Did everything come out okay?" Tobias asked.

"Huh?"

"You just went to the bathroom. It's a joke. I'm asking if everything came out okay. Get it? Came out?"

Zola let out a little snort. Men could be so unbelievably lame. It just showed that no one was perfect. Tobias had his nice side and he had his dork side. But so did all guys. She thought about her little brother, Nathaniel, and wondered if he'd grow up to have a dork side, too.

"Hey, Zo, thanks for going shopping with us," Tobias said, scratching Ozzy's head. "It was really cool of you."

Before she could respond, Zola's cell phone rang, and she answered it.

Surprise, it was Olivia. "Okay, I'm calling," she said.

"Hi, Olivia," Zola said with fake surprise.

"Uh, hi," Olivia said.

"Tobias, it's Olivia," Zola told Tobias.

"I figured," Tobias said.

"What? You're having trouble with a paper?" Zola asked. "Wait! Maybe Tobias can help!"

"What?" Tobias said.

"Tobias, Olivia is having trouble finishing her English extra-credit paper. If she doesn't get an A, she won't be valedictorian. She has to have it in by tomorrow morning and then they're announcing the valedictorian in the afternoon. This is really important. Do you think you could help her out? She could meet you over at the library, maybe? At the university?" Zola asked. She wished she had come up with a plan B in case he said no.

"No," Tobias said. He burped. "No fucking way."

Zola had to think fast. "It's on female sexuality," she said.

"No, it's not," Olivia said. "Gross. Don't give him any ideas."

"You could really help her out a lot, Tobias. You know, give her the male perspective," Zola said.

"You mean like answer questions about sex?" Tobias asked.

"Yes, definitely," Zola said.

"Graphic questions?"

Zola nodded enthusiastically.

"Uh, all right. Okay, why not?" Tobias said. He clutched his abdomen and burped again. "First I gotta get something to eat, though. I always get gassy when I don't eat."

"Great," Zola said, ignoring him. "He'll meet you at the library in a half hour. Shall we synchronize our watches?"

"Synchronize our watches?" Tobias asked. "What is this? *Mission Impossible III*?"

Zola had to admit that Tobias was a hell of a lot nicer than she had given him credit for, but let's face it, he was no Tom Cruise. Still, Zola was feeling a little confused about Operation Dump Tobias's Ass. She wondered if she should even say something to Min about it. She couldn't believe she had so drastically changed her mind since this morning.

Maybe this was all an impossible mission. But they had to at least try.

⑱

(Jane Austen)

Olivia, dressed in her most serious collegiate outfit, replete with glasses and plaid hair scrunchie, finally sat down at a round table facing the library elevators. She had spent about twenty minutes walking around trying to choose the table with the most visibility.

"Okay, are you sure this table is to your liking? Perhaps we can get the maître d' to show you another?" Tobias said, annoyed. "I can't believe after all that you chose the noisiest-possible table."

"I can't concentrate unless I'm facing in the exact right direction," Olivia said.

"That's ridiculous," Tobias said, leaning back in his chair.

"It's a sort of a feng shui thing with me," Olivia said.

"A what shwee?" Tobias asked.

"You know, feng shui," Olivia said. "The ancient Chinese art of arranging furniture so the chi travels in the right way and you get better luck. Like if your bed is facing so that when you're sleeping your head is facing east, you'll have a better love life."

"Bullshit!" Tobias said, smirking. "Where'd you hear that, *20/20*? And Min said you were smart!"

"Whatever." Olivia sighed. Tobias was being unsurprisingly thickheaded. She couldn't wait for Min to dump him.

Olivia craned her neck all around to look for Holden. The place was pretty empty. Disappointed, she took out her notes. Her paper was called "The Humor of Jane Austen," and she was supposed to point out the humor in three books, *Pride and Prejudice*, *Emma*, and *Persuasion*. She didn't even mind the topic because she really did like Jane Austen.

"If your paper is about kung phooey, I don't think I can help," Tobias said.

Olivia rolled her eyes and told him what the topic was.

"You're kidding, right?" he said.

"No," Olivia said.

Tobias crossed his arms and stuck out his lower lip, pouting like a little kid. "I thought the paper was about girls having sex," he whined.

Olivia suppressed a snigger. Boys could be so immature. "No, it's about humor," she said.

"Oh," Tobias said. He sounded so disappointed that

Olivia was suddenly nervous that he might want to leave.

"Well, it could be about sex, too," she said.

Tobias's eyes immediately lit up.

"I mean, when you think about it, sex is rather humorous," Olivia went on.

"Which part?" Tobias asked, genuinely interested.

"All of it. I mean, it's like the most basic, animal thing. And yet we play all these games with each other trying to get it. But then again, the games really have more to do with love than sex. Because when it comes down to it—and all of Jane Austen's books back this up—what we all want, what we truly want, more than sex, more than anything, is to be loved." Suddenly Olivia felt like Jennifer Grey in *Dirty Dancing,* pouring out her heart to Patrick Swayze.

Tobias squinted like his brain was on serious overload. "This is giving me a headache," he said.

He looked at Olivia's notes spread out on the table. "Wow, you're really serious about this, aren't you?" he said. "Why don't we just watch *Clueless* and call it a day? The chick in that movie is so damn hot."

The elevator dinged and the doors opened and Olivia held her breath. A girl and two guys got off, but Holden wasn't one of them.

"I've actually seen all those movies. Min loves that junk. *Emma* was the one where Gwyneth Paltrow was such a major bitch, right? And what's it called . . . *Mansfield Park*? There was some serious cleavage happening in that one. Hey, but I have to admit, I didn't totally hate them. I mean, Min loved them so much, the first thing she wanted to do when we turned the tape off was have sex. It was worth it."

"You saw all those movies?" Olivia asked, genuinely surprised. "I thought Ozzy hated chick flicks." It was something she'd heard Tobias say more than once.

"He does. But Min wanted to see them, and you know I can't say no to her. Ozzy just had to suck it up for once."

"Wow," Olivia said. "I thought you guys let Ozzy have his way no matter what."

Tobias shook his head. "That wouldn't be good parenting, would it?" he said, smiling. "Nah, Min wins out over Ozzy, no question."

"Wow," Olivia said again. Tobias was clearly very in love with Min. She wondered if Holden would ever talk about her the way Tobias talked about Min.

Tobias suddenly ducked his head under the table and then sat up, his eyes filled with panic. Ozzy was missing. They had both been so engrossed in their conversation, they hadn't noticed that he was gone. Tobias bolted out of his chair and started running up and down the aisles between the stacks, loudly whispering his name.

Olivia turned red just watching him. It was sweet that

Tobias cared so much about Min and about his dog. But there was no getting around the fact that he was a pathetic loser geek.

"Is there anything I can do to help?" Olivia asked when he ran past her.

"No. You better stay here in case he comes back to the table. When a child is lost, it's always best for one parent to stay in the same place so the child can find his way back," Tobias said.

"Okay," Olivia said, relieved. She really didn't want to run around the library after a dog. All those good-looking college boys might think she was some kind of freak.

The elevator doors opened again and Holden stepped out. Ozzy ran from behind the checkout desk and ducked into the elevator just as the doors slid shut.

Olivia was too stunned to do anything because there was Holden standing right in front of her.

"Hi, you," he said.

"Hi," she said back.

"Wait, don't tell me," he said, pointing his finger at her. "Olivia, right?"

"Right," she said, beaming. "And wait, don't tell me," she said, pointing her finger back at him. She couldn't just blurt out his name and let him know that she had been saying it in her head over and over again since they met. She felt like the writers of *The Rules* were perched on either one of her shoulders, cheering her on.

"You're . . . ," She hesitated, pretending to be stuck on his name.

"Holden," he said, looking a tiny bit let down. "Holden. I met you at the bookstore Sunday?"

"Right, I remember," Olivia said. "You're the future lawyer."

"Right," Holden said, perking up again. "What are you doing here?"

"I'm just helping a friend study," Olivia said casually.

"Oh?" Holden said. "Where is she?"

"*He's* over there somewhere," Olivia said.

Was it her imagination or did Holden look adorably jealous? *"Oh yeah!"* the writers of *The Rules* were shouting. *"You go, girl! He's all yours now!"*

"He's just the boyfriend of a friend of mine," Olivia added quickly. "And he's really a bit strange."

As if on cue, Tobias came running back to the table with sweat pouring down his face. "I can't find him," he gasped.

"Hello, Tobias," Holden said.

"Hey, Holden," Tobias said.

"You know each other?" Olivia said, startled beyond belief. How could two boys from completely different planets know each other?

"We're roommates," Holden said, looking uncomfortable.

"*Were* roommates," Tobias corrected, slapping Holden on the back. "Hey, dude, I'd like to hang out, but I gotta find my dog."

Olivia couldn't believe it. Roommates! Min had been to Tobias's dorm a million times. She never mentioned that he had a gorgeous roommate. Olivia couldn't believe her luck. Now she could grill Tobias about Holden and find out absolutely everything about him. But first she wanted Tobias to leave them alone so Holden could ask her out. "Ozzy got on the left elevator," she said. "I couldn't stop him."

"Up or down?" Tobias asked anxiously, running toward the elevators.

"Up, I think," Olivia said.

Tobias ran to the elevator and pressed the button. The doors opened right away and he got on.

"He really likes that dog," Holden said.

They both laughed.

Holden looked down at her paper. "Oh, Jesus, I *hate* Jane Austen," he said. "My last girlfriend dragged me to one of those movies, what was it, *Annie*?"

"*Emma,*" Olivia said.

"Right, *Emma.* That kind of movie just makes my ass ache."

"Yeah," Olivia said, but she was disappointed. For a moment she wondered if she actually had more in common with Tobias than she did with Holden.

"You know, Olivia, it sort of feels like fate that we met again, doesn't it?" Holden said. "We can't waste all this good karma. We should definitely go out for a drink sometime, don't you think?"

"Okay," Olivia said. She had never been asked out for a drink before. Of course she had sneaked into bars with Zola, but this was different. She would have to think about what drink to order.

"How about tomorrow night?" Holden asked.

"That sounds great," Olivia said. Her mother had her meditation group Wednesday nights, and her dad would be watching baseball with his friends from work, like he did all summer long. It would be no problem.

"Great," Holden said. "Why don't we meet at my dorm tomorrow night, say at seven?"

"Okay," Olivia said, noticing the chest hair sticking out of the neckline of his shirt. She wanted to touch it. "Seven's fine."

"You're pretty fine yourself," Holden said, giving her an approving once-over. "I'll see you tomorrow night."

Just then both elevators opened and Ozzy got off one and Tobias got off the other. They ran to each other. As silly as it was, Olivia couldn't help thinking that any man who looked that happy to be reunited with his dog couldn't be all that bad.

Holden gave a little thumbs-up sign and went into the computer room. Tobias sat down at the table with Ozzy in his arms, exhausted.

"Bad, bad boy," he whispered, giggling, as Ozzy covered his face with little doggy tongue kisses.

Olivia watched them for a minute, bursting with questions to ask Tobias about Holden.

"So, I can't believe Holden's your roommate!" she exclaimed.

"Yeah," Tobias said, giving her a quizzical look. "Wait, you have a crush on him, don't you?"

"Very perceptive," Olivia said, smiling and blushing happily.

"That's cool," Tobias said.

"Really?" Olivia said, surprised. "I was sure you were going to tell me all sorts of horrible things about him."

"Nah," Tobias said. "He's an okay dude. We just got on each other's nerves living together, that's all."

"Is he seeing anyone?" Olivia asked.

"I don't think he's seeing anyone special," Tobias said. "But he does date lots of girls. I don't think he's really the boyfriend type."

"Uh-huh," Olivia said. Or maybe Holden just hadn't met the right girlfriend yet, she thought.

"I thought you were dating that science geek," Tobias said.

"Biology Bill," Olivia said guiltily. "Well, no. We were never really dating. We just kind of fool around sometimes." She sighed. "I don't know."

"It doesn't sound like you're all that into him," Tobias said. "Maybe it would be better not to fool around with him, then. It's kind of like eating when you're not hungry."

Olivia nodded thoughtfully. She was really grateful to Tobias for being so up-front and honest with her and so . . . wise. She had never talked about boys with a boy before. It was fascinating.

"So, what's Holden's favorite drink?" Olivia asked.

"Milk," Tobias answered.

"Milk?" she said. "No, I mean what does he order when he goes to a bar?"

"Milk," Tobias repeated. "That's one of the reasons I can't live with the guy. He only drinks milk."

"Well," Olivia said, laughing. "You know what the ad says, 'It does a body good'? It's definitely done Holden's body good."

"Yeah," Tobias said. "But don't let the milk thing fool you; he is kind of a player. I'm just being completely honest here."

"Thanks, Tobias," Olivia said.

"The important thing is to be yourself," Tobias said.

"What's that supposed to mean?" Olivia asked. "Who else could I be?"

"You know what I mean. You don't have to like milk just because he does. That sort of thing. Guys like girls with minds of their own."

Olivia listened carefully.

"You know, it's been kind of cool hanging out with you and Zola today," Tobias said. "Min's never really let us all hang out together. Maybe we should all go to a movie this weekend or something."

"Sure, Tobias," Olivia said. She felt terrible. By the weekend Tobias was going to be history. She couldn't even remember why they were so against Tobias in the first place. As far as she could tell, now that she had actually spent some time with him, his only real fault was that he was a little perverted when it came to his dog. But even Ozzy wasn't so bad. He was kind of cute, licking Tobias's chin. She wondered if they were doing the right thing, encouraging Min to go out with Myles.

This whole situation was very Jane Austen.

⑲

(Fatal Attraction)

Shopping with Tobias had made Zola miss Evan so much, she couldn't think about anything else. The more she thought about it, the more she became convinced that the whole situation could really be fixed if she could just talk to him and tell him that she loved him. This was ridiculous. She was going back to his house.

She had been so distracted that she hadn't even noticed that the gas gauge on her car was below empty. Her car ran out of gas about three blocks from Evan's house. It was just her luck. Her whole life was really becoming pathetic.

Zola got out of her stupid car and walked to Evan's house. His car was in the driveway, alone. Claudia's car wasn't there, thank God, and neither were his parents' cars. Zola would finally be able to talk to him.

She walked up to the front door, knocked, and stood there, waiting nervously. "Why are you so nervous?" she asked herself. "It's just Evan. Your boyfriend." Well, *ex*-boyfriend, but hopefully not ex for long.

Great, this was all she needed, to be caught talking to herself like a nut.

But Evan didn't come to the door. She waited a while longer and then walked around to the side of the house and looked in the living-room window. There was no one there. Just Evan's Puma running shoes on the living-room rug. She had spent so many hours with Evan in that living room, on that couch, watching TV and making out. She felt like it was practically her home, too.

Zola went around to the back door. Evan was either in the kitchen or he was upstairs in his room. She looked into the kitchen through the screen door. She saw the refrigerator she had opened a million times, the framed chili peppers poster over the kitchen table, the neatly lined up boxes of cereal on the counter.

Zola knew that the Fells didn't lock the back door until they went to bed at night. Without thinking, she let herself into the kitchen. "Evan," she called out. He didn't answer. Maybe he wasn't there after all. He might have gone off with one of his parents.

All of a sudden Zola was very thirsty. She got a glass out of the cabinet and filled it with ice chips from the ice dispenser and water from the filtered water spout. She sat down at the kitchen table and drank, sighing deeply when she was done. She felt calm. Just being there in his house again made her feel better. She felt close to him again.

Zola closed her eyes for a minute and breathed deeply.

"Breaking and entering. Ten to twenty in the state prison," she heard a man say.

Zola jumped out of her seat, spilling ice water all over herself. It was Clarence Terence. "You scared the shit out of me," she said.

"What are you doing here?" Clarence asked. "You're really trying to get yourself in trouble, aren't you?"

"It's not what it looks like," Zola said. "I just wanted to talk to Evan."

"Then why did you park three blocks away and sneak in through the back door when he isn't even home?"

Clarence took a giant pot off the counter and handed it to Zola. It had a rabbit in it. A live rabbit.

"What the hell are you doing now?" Zola asked.

"Well, you looked like you were doing your best Glenn Close impression, so I thought I'd help you out," Clarence said.

"This is not *Fatal Attraction*," Zola said.

"Well, then stop acting like a psycho," Clarence said.

"Look, Lenny, you're the one acting like a psycho," Zola said. "First you show up with pig's blood, then a live rabbit in a pot."

"Isn't he cute?" Clarence said. The rabbit was light sandy brown with a white tail. Clarence picked it up and held it, and it nestled comfortably in his arms. "See how if you handle him gently, he isn't even scared?"

"Are you trying to say I should handle Evan gently?" Zola asked.

"I'm saying you have to be sensitive. You made a mistake. You were the one who hurt Evan first. You've broken his trust and now you have to win it back. You have to find a way to apologize that doesn't involve criminal behavior like breaking and entering or hacking into computers," Clarence said. "You'll just have to find some other way to show him you care about him."

But Zola had stopped listening. Lenny had given her a fantastic idea. His computer! Evan kept a journal on his computer. If she could just get up to his room and into his computer, maybe she could find out how he really felt about Claudia. And how he felt about her, too. But she couldn't do it now, not with Lenny there.

"You're right," Zola said to keep him quiet. "Hey, can I keep the rabbit?"

"For what?" Clarence asked suspiciously.

"To give to my brother; what do you think I want him for?" Zola said. God, he really did think she was a psycho. "Nathaniel will love this little guy. We'll call him Lenny."

"All right, but take good care of him," Clarence said. "Bye-bye, Lenny," he whispered into the rabbit's long pink ear.

"Bye, Lenny," Zola whispered into Clarence's.

"Oh, and by the way, dear," Clarence said to Zola. "Your tank's full."

Zola smiled gratefully.

"Aren't you going to *tank* me?" Clarence said.

"Tanks a lot," Zola said.

Zola, Lenny, and Lenny the rabbit left the Fells' house just as Mrs. Fell's car pulled into the driveway.

(20)

(Current Events)

While Min was getting ready for her date with Myles, Sally was getting ready for her turn with Tobias. Sally was supposed to meet Tobias at La Lantern, a French restaurant not far from the campus. Sally thought it was a terrible idea. Tobias was expecting *Min* to show up for a romantic dinner, not her. What was she supposed to say? "Oh, sorry, Tobias, Min couldn't make it, so I guess you have to treat me to dinner instead"?

Sally opened her book, titled *How to Act Like an Interesting Person.* She opened to the chapter called "The Art of Conversation" and began to read.

> *To kick start a conversation with some- one you are just getting to know, you should start with the basics: where he grew up, his schooling, and his profession. Ask questions in a neutral fashion, such as, "Was your*

mother a good cook?" or, "Did you learn to play an instrument?" Be sure to follow up with affirmative remarks, such as, "That is certainly an honorable profession," or, "That must have required a lot of special training."

Remember the way to be an interesting person is to be interested. Don't speak about yourself, following every question with comments such as, "My mother is a terrible cook; you should have tasted her spaghetti," or, "I had piano lessons, but I never really took to them." Follow your questions with more questions, not boring stories of your own.

At dinner it is important never to make references to anything unpleasant such as blood, gore, disease, bodily functions, and so on. One should also avoid discussing religion, politics, and the weather.

It is a good idea, however, to read the local newspaper before any social occasion so you can appear to be abreast of interesting current events and join in conversations more easily.

At the word *abreast* Sally blushed, remembering her recent television humiliation. This wasn't going to work.

She looked around for a newspaper, but there weren't any in her house. She turned on CNN while she finished getting ready. She had to have something to talk to Tobias about.

Unfortunately, the story being broadcast was about how breast augmentation was more popular than ever. "There are two shape options for implants," the news-caster was saying. "Round and anatomical." What on earth was anatomical? She turned the television back off. Why was the whole world obsessed with breasts? That was the last thing in the world Sally wanted to talk to Tobias about.

Sally wondered if Min was still at home. She called and Min answered. "Um, I can't really talk now, Sally," Min said. "Myles just got here."

"Sorry," Sally said. "But I'm not sure about this. I don't think Tobias and I are going to have anything to say to each other."

"Then don't say anything," Min said.

"What are we supposed to do, just stare at each other?" Sally asked.

"Don't worry, Sally, it's no big deal. If you're having a bad time, just tell him you're not feeling well and leave. And you can always talk about Ozzy. Ask Tobias to show you his puppy pictures."

"He has puppy pictures?" Sally asked, horrified.

"Sure. We both do. I keep mine in my date book, with my old concert ticket stubs," Min answered. "Remember when we went to see Beck and those guys wanted us to dance on the hood of their car for them? That was scary."

Their conversation continued like that for a few minutes until Min thanked Sally for saving her life, and they hung up. Sally left the house, grabbing the book to read at red lights for any last minute tips.

(Spirituality)

"Sorry about the phone," Min said to Myles. He had shown up right on time for their date, and he looked even more handsome than she remembered him. He really reminded her of someone, but she couldn't put her finger on it. When she turned around and saw him sprawled out on her couch wearing dark rinse jeans and funky leather boots, she realized who he looked like. Clarence Terence.

Min's parents were at the synagogue, so they were alone. She sat down next to Myles on the couch.

"What were you thinking about just now?" Min asked.

"I don't know if I should say," Myles said.

"Tell me," Min said.

"Well, I'm not particularly proud of myself for thinking this," Myles said. "But if you really want to know, I was trying to conjure up all my telepathic powers to cause a major power outage in the area."

Min laughed. That wasn't exactly what she was expecting him to say.

"Why were you hoping for a power outage?" she asked.

"Because I was hoping the phone lines would go down so that you'd be disconnected and we could start our date."

Min smiled. "Well, I don't think the phone lines have anything to do with the power lines. But we can start our date anytime."

Myles looked at the gold menorah on the bookshelf. "So you're Jewish?" Myles asked.

"Yeah," Min said. "My dad is a rabbi." She knew this fact always intimidated boys. "But he's pretty cool." Actually her dad wasn't all that cool when it came to boys, but she didn't want to scare him. "Like he adopted me even though he knew my birth mother wasn't Jewish. He doesn't care about stuff like that. He's not strict or anything."

"That's cool," Myles said. "I'm really interested in different religions. Well, not religions exactly, but spirituality. I've been reading this book called *Zen and the Art of Motorcycle Maintenance*."

Wow, now he was really reminding Min of Clarence. But in a cute way. It was so sexy just hearing him say words like *Zen* and *spirituality*.

"Should we get going?" she asked. She didn't want her parents to come home and find them, and if Sally was having trouble with Tobias, Min wanted to be out of the house in case he came back there.

Myles nodded, lapping her up with his gaze. "You know what?" he asked.

"What?" Min said. She felt like she was the girl in a Lenny Kravitz song—all hot and sexy and womanly.

"I think I'm going to really like living in Madison."

(21)

(The Art of Conversation)

Tobias sat at La Lantern in a romantic corner banquette, waiting for Min. He was feeling a little nervous for some reason. Min hadn't really been herself lately. She had been acting distant and they had been bickering like an old married couple. He figured it had to do with the pressure of the prom, and finals, and graduation. Anyway, now they could finally be alone, just the three of them.

He tore off a piece of baguette, buttered it, and fed it to Ozzy, who was nestled happily in Tobias's fishing hat in the You're the Man shopping bag. Ozzy loved French food. Tobias had decided to surprise Min by changing into his new suit and doggy tie. Even though he was still wearing his bright green ripped sneakers, he looked pretty sharp if he did say so himself.

Tobias was ready to have a serious talk with Min about the future. She was graduating high school now.

He was going to suggest that they find an apartment near the campus and move in together.

His thoughts were interrupted by Min's friend Sally standing at the table. "Hi, Tobias," she said.

"Hi, Sally," he said.

"Min couldn't make it," Sally said woodenly. She sounded like she was reading off a script. "Zola got sick and Min had to go help her."

"I just saw Zola. She seemed fine to me," Tobias said. "Jesus, I should really get a cell phone. And Min has to stop using her friends as carrier pigeons. Hey, why didn't she just call me here at the restaurant?"

Sally froze. She hadn't thought of that. "Uh, I guess she thought you'd want to have dinner with someone and she felt really bad about standing you up."

Tobias started to stand up. "Well, that's all right, Sal; thanks for letting me know. I'll just head back to Min's house and wait for her."

"No!" Sally shrieked, alarmed. What if Min was still home with Myles? She had to keep Tobias there. Boldly she sat down and slid into the banquette next to him. "Where did you grow up?" she blurted out. "Was your mother a good cook? Did you learn to play an instrument?"

Tobias looked at Sally like she was crazy. "Uh, I grew up in Chicago and my mother was an excellent cook if you consider Chef Boyardee a delicacy. And drums. I used to play the drums."

Sally desperately tried to think of a follow-up question. She was on overload. She couldn't concentrate on anything he had just said. "What is your profession?" she asked, like a crazed conversation-making robot.

"My profession? I'm a college student. Duh. I thought you knew that."

"That certainly is an honorable profession," Sally said.

"Sally, are you feeling all right?" Tobias asked.

"Of course," Sally said. "Why do you ask?"

"Well, you're sweating and you look like you're about to puke."

Now what was she supposed to do? He was bringing up gross bodily functions. This conversation was not going well.

"No, I'm fine," Sally said. "I'm just trying to get to know you better. I'm really interested in you."

"Really?" Tobias asked.

Sally nodded and took a gulp of water.

The waitress came over, wielding her little pad. "What can I get for you?" she asked.

"I'm not sure if we're going to be staying," Tobias said.

"I'll have the mixed-green salad and the chicken Alsace," Sally said quickly. "And a bottle of red wine."

"A bottle of red wine?" Tobias said, laughing. "Uh, I

guess we are staying," he told the waitress. He ordered the snapper and a beer. "And I think Sally will have a *glass* of red wine. For a start," he added.

Sally felt incredibly relieved. She had kept the conversation going well enough to keep Tobias interested in having dinner with her.

"You know, Sally," Tobias said. "It's funny that you mentioned instruments. It's been a long time since I thought about playing the drums. I used to have my own drum set. A pearl gray Slingerland with Zildjian cymbals. It was so cool. I loved that kit. I remember when my dad bought it for me. I never thought he'd let me have it in a million years, and when I asked him and told him this kid in my school was selling a great set, he just pulled out his wallet and handed me the three hundred bucks. I couldn't believe it. It was just about the nicest thing the old man ever did for me. I used to play in my room every day after school. Then one day I came home and saw him sitting on the stool, holding the sticks and banging away like crazy, like he thought he was a rock star or something. We both started laughing really hard. I'm not sure what exactly was so funny about it, but we both really cracked up laughing. I hocked the set when I came to college. I should really get another one, though. I'm glad you brought it up."

Sally didn't know what to say. The book was right. If

you asked enough questions, the other person would just keep talking. She had to think of more questions. The waitress brought their drinks and they each took a sip. There was a lull in the conversation. Then she remembered current events. "Did you know that breast augmentation is more popular than ever?" she asked.

Tobias spit out his beer. "What?"

"Do you prefer a round-shaped implant or an anatomical shape?"

"An anatomical shape?" Tobias asked. "Is this some kind of test? Did Min ask you to ask me this? I like whatever shape she is. But I have to say, Sally, you did look pretty good in that bra you were wearing on TV."

Sally felt herself turn bright red. Tobias wasn't being obnoxious. He was paying her a genuine compliment. "Really?" she asked.

"Yeah," he said. "Excellent ta-tas."

"Ew," Sally said, but she was secretly pleased. She took a sip of wine and stuck out her chest just a tiny bit.

"You know, Sally, you're definitely a hottie," Tobias said.

"A hottie?" Sally asked, completely shocked. "Me?"

"Yeah, you're a babe. Min says you're really shy with guys, but I don't know why you would be. Min always says how pretty Zola is, but if you ask me, you're definitely Min's cutest friend. And you're really easy to talk to. I was just thinking about some of the things you said tonight, and you're right—being a college student *is* an honorable profession. I never actually thought about it that way. I know a lot of kids from La Follette who didn't even go to college, and they're just living with their parents and working some shitty job. It is an honorable thing to pursue a higher education."

Sally had never felt so happy in her entire life. She was thrilled. She was so high up on cloud nine, she hadn't noticed the waitress put their plates of food down on the table in front of them. This must be what it's like to be on a date, Sally thought. A wonderful date with a man.

She took a bite of her chicken. "Would you like to try this?" she asked.

Tobias said that he would. Sally cut a piece and leaned over and actually fed the chicken to Tobias on her fork. She *fed* him like it was a scene in a romantic movie. She was like Meg Ryan feeding Tom Hanks in a real restaurant.

"Mmmm, it's good," Tobias said. Sally took her napkin and wiped the corners of Tobias's mouth. She couldn't believe herself! His mouth didn't even have any food on it; she just felt like doing it.

Then, before she could stop herself, Sally kissed

Tobias. She just closed her eyes, leaned forward, and did it. He tasted like beer. Her right breast was touching his left arm. "Oh, Tobias," she said.

"Whoa! Down, girl," Tobias said. He pushed her away gently and brushed the hair off her cheek. "Sally," he said. "I'm in love with Min."

"I know," Sally said quickly. She was embarrassed.

"I think the wine went to your head."

Sally nodded miserably. What a complete disaster. Why did she have to go and ruin things like that? But it wasn't all her fault. If anything, it was Min's fault. Suddenly she had the urge to blurt everything out and tell Tobias that all of this was just a ploy to get rid of him. What had she been thinking? Did she think Tobias would take her back to his apartment and rip off all her clothes and devirginize her? She should have just asked to look at puppy pictures and left it at that.

"I'm sorry," Sally said. "I don't know what . . ."

"Let's forget about it, Sal. We're having a great time. The kiss will be our secret. Let's just finish our dinner and keep talking. But I don't know what Min was talking about. You're not shy at all. You're the horniest girl I've ever seen, and you're an excellent kisser."

Sally felt instantly better. A great kisser!

"Sally, do you ever think about your future?" Tobias asked.

"Actually, I've been thinking about that a lot lately," she said, giggling. She couldn't believe she was sitting there flirting and having a great time with a man, even if it was only Tobias. She was even kind of glad she had kissed him. Maybe she would try to date Tobias after Min finished breaking up with him.

(22)

(Karma Chameleon)

"So this is the romantic restaurant you're taking me to?" Min asked. She would have been happy to go anyplace (except La Lantern), but this was absolutely perfect.

"That's right," Myles said. He helped her onto the small boat, untied the rope from the dock, and got in after her. Then he started the motor with some impressive, manly pulls on the starter cord. They didn't talk until they were a good distance into the middle of the lake and Myles turned off the motor.

"I hope you like turkey sandwiches," he said, unpacking the picnic basket. "I hear turkey is full of endorphins. It makes you sleepy."

"Yum," Min said, taking a sandwich. She wouldn't mind feeling sleepy with Myles. Not at all.

They sat in the boat, under the full moon, eating the sandwiches.

"Do you get high?" Myles asked.

"Not really," Min said. "I mean, I *have*." Actually she never had, but this was the line she always used. She knew pot gave people the munchies and that was the last thing in the world she needed. She had a hard enough time not eating everything in sight without chemical enhancement.

"Do you mind if I do?" Myles asked.

Min shrugged. Myles lit a joint and took a drag. "You know, marijuana has been used medicinally for centuries."

The smell of the pot reminded Min of Tobias. He was never a stoner, but now and then he used to roll up a joint while they were watching a movie. He'd stopped soon after they got Ozzy because he didn't want the dog to breathe in any harmful secondhand smoke. Min wondered what the two of them were doing at that exact moment in time.

A million things were running through Min's head. She was especially worried about poor Sally. Min knew Sally would rather endure going to the gynecologist than have dinner alone with Tobias. And that was saying a lot. She really had the greatest friends in the world.

Myles offered Min the joint and she took it. She was so tense, worrying about Tobias. She thought maybe it would relax her. She took a drag and tried not to cough, but of course she did.

They passed the joint back and forth a few times. Min could feel the effect right away. She felt fuzzy and light and whirring, like she was electrically charged.

Myles moved a little closer to her and leaned his face in to hers. Slowly, slowly they brought their lips closer and closer together until they were almost touching. Min parted her lips slightly and then he kissed her. Kissing him seemed so odd to Min, she felt like laughing. It was strange to be kissing another man. She was so used to Tobias, his stubbly chin and dog shampoo smell. Myles was smooth and smelled like Hellmann's mayonnaise from the sandwiches.

"There," Myles said. "The first kiss. I'm glad we got that out of the way. I couldn't concentrate on our conversation. Now we can just kick back and enjoy ourselves."

"Uh-huh," Min answered vaguely. She had been so busy comparing Myles to Tobias, she hadn't even really felt the kiss.

She thought about her pregnancy scare the day before and how different things would be if she had really been pregnant with Tobias's baby. Life was so crazy. You never knew what was going to happen. She wondered if Myles would be a part of her future now and what would have happened if they had never met. If he hadn't randomly appeared at lunchtime yesterday. Or if his mother had never met his father and he had never been born.

"You really should read that book I told you about," Myles said. "It's made me think a lot about karma. Meeting you, that felt, you know, like good karma."

Min didn't even hear him. She was thinking about what she was going to say to Tobias. How she was going to break it to him that they didn't have a future together. She would do it tonight. As soon as she got home she would go downstairs to the rec room and tell him.

I don't want us to be a couple anymore, she would say. I want to break up. I love you, but I'm not in love with you. We're in a rut. We need to take a break. It's over. Min pictured the whole conversation in her head. She knew exactly how it would happen.

Her thoughts were suddenly interrupted by the sound of a motor. Some kind of patrol boat was going by.

"Is everything okay out there?" she heard a voice boom through a PA system.

Myles quickly stubbed out the joint and stood up.

"Everything's fine," he shouted back, cupping his hands around his mouth.

Min couldn't believe this was happening. Her mind was a jumble of confused, panicked thoughts. She was sure they were going to get arrested for the pot and they'd have to spend the night in jail and then her parents would have to find out. It might even be in the papers and then Tobias would find out. It was only two weeks until graduation and she could be suspended over this. She might not graduate. It served her right for sneaking around behind Tobias's back. It was karma, as Myles would say. And Clarence. She had given herself bad karma because she was a big fat cheating liar.

"Is the young lady all right?" the voice from the boat asked.

Min jumped to her feet. "I'm fine! Yes! Perfectly fine!" she called, waving vigorously and making a stupid thumbs-up sign.

"You kids better head back," the voice boomed.

Myles waved again and started the motor, heading the boat back to shore. The patrol boat went off in the opposite direction. Min wasn't sure if the pot was making her see things, but she could almost swear that she saw the name *Karma Chameleon* on the side of the boat.

(The Art of Conversation II)

After dinner Tobias and Sally decided they wanted ice cream. It turned out mint chocolate chip in a sugar cone was both of their favorites.

Sally and Tobias walked along the lake, eating their cones and not really saying much. Ozzy scampered at their feet, peeing and sniffing wherever he saw fit. Sally was beginning to catch on that you didn't have to make nonstop conversation with a man. You could have some quiet time, too. She looked at her watch. It was already ten o'clock, and it was a school night. She wasn't going to get any sleep tonight, she realized. She didn't know when she'd get home, and then she'd have to sit up in bed for at least an hour or two so she could write all of this down in her diary. It definitely couldn't wait until tomorrow.

"I guess you probably want to get back, Sal," Tobias said.

"No," Sally said.

"I saw you look at your watch."

"I don't want to go home yet," Sally said. "Let's just sit on this bench for a few minutes."

They sat on a bench by the water, but as soon as they did Sally regretted it more than she had ever regretted anything in her whole life because there, on the dock in front of them, were Min and Myles in a major lip lock.

Sally jumped up. "Uh, actually I really should get going." Tobias hadn't spotted Min yet. There was still a chance to distract him. Sally let go of her ice-cream cone, and it splattered on the ground. "God, I'm such a klutz," she shrieked. "Come on." She tugged at Tobias's suit jacket.

"Sally, what's wrong?" Tobias said.

Sally was afraid to look in the direction of Min and Myles again, so she looked up at the sky. "Isn't the moon beautiful?" she said.

"Sally . . ." Suddenly Tobias stopped talking. Sally looked at him. He was staring right at Min. Sally wondered what was going through Tobias's head as he watched his girlfriend kissing this complete stranger.

"So this is the reason for the three surprise visits from the musketeers—Zola, Olivia, and you. Now I get it. The Charlie's Angels of dating," Tobias said, his voice filled with rage. "You were tricking me! Covering for that bitch."

Sally felt like crying. No book in the world could have prepared her for this conversation. She felt like it was all her fault. She should have just gone right home after dinner.

Tobias walked up to Min and Myles, who were still kissing. Sally stood next to her ice-cream mess, unable to move. She felt terrible for Min, and Tobias, and even herself. This was horrible. And there was nothing anyone could do.

(23)
(The Breakup)

The breakup was nothing like Min had planned. There were no *I love you, but I'm not in love with you*s. There were no lingering teary hugs and promises to be friends forever. There was no exchange of each other's property—the books she had lent him, the shirts of his she had worn home. No gently wiping the tears from each other's faces.

All there was was a lot of yelling. Min had never seen Tobias so angry.

"You slut! You cheating bitch," he screamed. "Is this that Clarence Terence character you were talking about?"

"Tobias, please stop," Min said. "Let me explain."

"Uncle Clarence?" Myles asked.

"What?" Min said. She was so confused.

"My name is Myles," Myles said, holding his hand out for Tobias to shake. "Take it easy, man."

Tobias glared at Myles disgustedly. "Who else are you fooling around with?" he yelled at Min.

"Tobias, I've wanted to talk to you for a long time," Min said.

"Yeah, well, there's no need to talk," Tobias shouted. "I have to get an AIDS test tomorrow. You're probably sleeping with all of Madison."

"Hey—," Myles said, coming to Min's defense. She had started crying next to him. He put his arm around her. "Why do you have to be this way?" he asked Tobias.

"You stay out of this," Tobias screamed, putting his face right into Myles's face. He looked like he was about to punch him.

"Stop it, Tobias," Min wailed. "You're scaring Lady M."

"I can't believe you would do this to me," Tobias said, softly this time with tears in his eyes.

"Enough already," Myles said.

"Enough?" Tobias asked, reeling toward Myles. "Enough? Is this enough?" He pulled his arm back and slugged Myles in the face. Myles fell backward and hit his head on the wooden dock. He lay there, moaning, blood pouring from his nose.

Tobias stormed off, glaring at Sally as he went. Sally stood there paralyzed, like a deer in front of a car.

Min squatted next to Myles. "Call an ambulance," she shouted at Sally.

But there was no need because just then an ambulance appeared out of nowhere. Two paramedics strapped Myles to a gurney so that his head was secure in case he had a broken neck and loaded him into the back of the ambulance.

"We can only take one of you," one of the men said to Min and Sally.

"I'll meet you there," Sally said.

Min climbed into the back of the ambulance with Myles. Sally watched as they drove off with the lights flashing and the siren blaring. She was trembling.

"All right, show's over," Clarence Terence said, coming up and putting his arm around her. Thank God he had been there to call for an ambulance. Sally looked like she had gone into shock.

He was beginning to wonder if he wasn't the worst fairy godmother and the worst great-grand-uncle in the universe. All he'd wanted was for Min to have a good time with another boy and for Myles to stick around so he could complete his destiny. Was that so wrong?

One thing was for sure—he was signing that kid up for boxing lessons just as soon as he was up on his feet again. In this world you needed more than a fairy godmother watching over you. You had to be able to help yourself from time to time.

(The Art of Conversation III)

In the hospital a very groggy Myles smiled sheepishly at Min and Sally. "I guess I wasn't very good protection," he said.

"I'm so sorry, Myles," Min said. "I was planning on telling him as soon as I got home. I had no idea he would see us and freak out like that."

"I know," Myles said.

The doctor began to bandage his broken nose. "You're a lucky boy," he said.

"What's so lucky about getting punched in the face by a crazed lunatic and having your damn nose broken?" Myles asked.

The doctor laughed. "You have a point," he said. "But a person can die from being punched in the nose. A bone can be pushed up from the nose into the brain and cause a hemorrhage."

Sally knew she shouldn't be thinking this, but she

couldn't help but notice that the doctor was handsome, in an older, tennis pro sort of way. His name tag said Dr. Bruce. She thought she'd try to make a little conversation.

"Where did you grow up?" she asked.

"New York City," the doctor said.

"Was your mother a good cook?" Sally asked.

"Sally, have you lost your marbles?" Min hissed.

"Actually, Sally, she was a great cook," Dr. Bruce said. "Still is. You wouldn't believe her apple pie. It's amazing."

"I think medicine is a very honorable profession," Sally said.

"Thank you, Sally," Dr. Bruce said. Then he actually winked at her!

"Sally, would you mind not bothering the doctor?" Min said, obviously annoyed.

"She's not bothering me at all," Dr. Bruce said. "I can clean up a broken nose and have an interesting conversation at the same time."

"Sally, can I talk to you in the hall for a minute?" Min said.

Sally followed Min into the hall. "What are you doing?" Min whispered.

"I'm flirting," Sally said.

"Do you think this is the right time to flirt?" Min asked.

"I'm sorry," Sally said, suddenly ashamed of herself. "I feel terrible about everything that's happened, I really do."

Just then they saw Clarence Terence walking toward them wearing a ridiculous pink-striped dress, his guitar strapped to his back.

"Lenny, what are you supposed to be now?" Min asked.

"I'm a candy striper," Clarence said, looking hurt. "And don't call me Lenny. I have a ginger ale for Myles."

"We really don't have time right now for games," Min said. "We'd really appreciate being left alone."

"Well, I would really appreciate you trying not to get each other killed," Clarence said. "You won't have much of a future if you're all dead. Then you'll have to do what I do, run around helping ungrateful teenagers."

"We'll be careful," Sally said.

"Thank you, Sally," Clarence said. "And stay away from Octopus Bruce. He's much too old for you."

"Lenny, you sound jealous," Sally said.

"Do you think being a fairy godmother is an honorable profession, Sally?" Clarence teased.

Sally didn't say anything.

"I should get back to Myles," Min said, taking the ginger ale. "Sally, why don't you call Zola and Olivia and tell them what's happened? They're not going to believe this."

"Okay," Sally said. Great. She sure had a lot of explaining to do. Everything had been fine until it was her turn to watch Tobias. Her friends were going to have a field day with this.

"Fine. I'm going to the maternity ward to hold some babies," Clarence said. "I love babies. And they love it when I play guitar for them."

Finally Dr. Bruce said it was okay to take Myles home, and Min and Sally walked him out of the hospital.

A paramedic wheeled a gurney past them in the parking lot, and Min and Sally noticed that the person lying on it was covered with a sheet. Even the person's head was covered. That meant he was dead. Min and Sally looked at each other, and suddenly the meaning of the moment hit them. The fight had been serious. Tobias could have killed Myles.

Here was a human being passing in front of them, lying dead on a stretcher. Dead! Life was so fragile. They looked at the form under the sheet. That could be one of them at any time.

Suddenly the dead man on the stretcher sat up and pulled the sheet off of himself. Min and Sally both screamed.

It was Lenny.

"Gotcha," he said, throwing back his head and laughing.

(24)

(You're Free!)

Even though it was midnight and everyone was exhausted, Zola insisted that Min, Olivia, and Sally all get together for a little sleep-over party. And the best and only place for that was Min's rec room. It was pretty clear that Tobias wouldn't be staying there any longer.

They had a lot to talk about. And even though it seemed strange, they had something to celebrate. Min had changed her future. She had broken up with Tobias once and for all.

They had to throw Min a You're Free party.

Zola had even bought a cake. She had convinced the old baker at Dough-Ray-Me to write *You're Free* on a chocolate cake in pink icing.

"You want I should hide a saw in the cake?" the baker said.

"Huh?" Zola said.

"You're free?" he said. "It sounds like you're bringing this cake to somebody in the clink."

Everyone was a comedian.

Zola, Olivia, and Sally sat staring at Min in her rec room, eating the cake. It wasn't much of a party. Everyone looked miserable.

"Thanks for the party," Min said through a mouthful of cake. She'd gotten the munchies, and despite everything that had happened, the cake tasted like heaven.

The other three girls looked at Tobias's duffel bag in the corner of the room and Ozzy's bones, stuffed animals, and squeeze toys scattered around on the beige carpet.

"Don't you want to hear about my date with Myles?" Min said. "It was the best first date I've ever had. He's amazing," she said. "I really like him."

"That's great, Min," Zola said halfheartedly.

Olivia picked up a toy hot dog that squeaked. "I feel bad for Tobias," she said.

"I know," Zola said. "He's actually a really great guy. I never realized until today."

Olivia and Sally both nodded in agreement.

"What!" Min said. "You all hated Tobias."

"He was really nice to me today," Olivia said.

"The guy's a lunatic," Min said. "He beat Myles up."

"I thought it was kind of romantic," Sally said. "I'd love to have two hunky men fighting over me."

"Since when do you think Tobias is a hunk?" Min asked.

"He is kind of a hunk," Zola said. "Did you see him in his suit?"

"You called him Tub-ass," Min said, exasperated. "I always told you he was a great guy, but you never believed me."

"We never really got to know him," Sally said.

"He called me a slut!" Min said, trying to rack up points against Tobias.

"Well . . . ," Olivia began, but then Zola nudged her and she shut up.

"Well, what?" Min challenged her.

"Never mind," Olivia mumbled.

They all sat silently eating their sad cake.

Min's father knocked on the door to the basement and Min yelled, "Come in."

"Where's Tobias?" Rabbi Weinstock asked.

"We broke up, Dad," Min said.

"Why?" her father asked. "What happened? Should I talk to him?"

"No, you shouldn't talk to him. I thought you'd be glad we broke up," Min said.

"I was really starting to like him," Rabbi Weinstock said, sounding disappointed. "I even liked having that little Ozzy fellow running around. I made Mrs. Greenspan promise to give me first pick of his puppies."

"That's nice, Dad," Min said tiredly. What was wrong with everyone?

Min's father kissed her on the forehead and told them not to stay up too late. Then he left them alone in the basement.

"Well, I think it's for the best," Min said, but she didn't sound convinced. "I wish Lenny would come back and show me my future again. It would be kind of reassuring to have an update."

"I doubt he's really going to be willing to show us our futures every day," Zola said. "But it would be great. Can you imagine? You wake up every morning, eat a bowl of corn flakes, and see your future. You could turn on the TV and Regis would show it to you. That way you'd know how to schedule your day."

"I couldn't take it," Sally said. "It's too depressing."

"Yeah," Olivia said. "It's depressing enough watching Regis without him showing my future."

"This sucks," Min said. "I'm dying to tell you about my boat ride with Myles and kissing him and everything and all you guys want to do is talk about Regis? Let's just go to sleep." At least then she could lie in bed and think about Myles and try not to think about Tobias.

"What are you complaining about?" Zola asked. "You're the one who actually managed to change your future. The rest of us haven't made an ounce of progress at all." Well, maybe an *ounce,* she thought, reconsidering. She hadn't killed Claudia yet, but she had broken into the computer at school and messed with her grades. That must be worth something. And as soon as she got the chance she was going to sneak into Evan's room and read his computer diary.

Olivia was thinking about her own progress. She'd completely changed the thesis for her extra-credit paper after talking with Tobias. She was going to write about sex and love, and she intended to wake up at the crack of dawn to finish it. Plus she had a date lined up with Holden. What all that meant exactly, she didn't know.

Sally felt like she had made a lot of progress. She had learned the secret to engaging men in conversation. She was learning how to flirt. She had been called an excellent kisser. She had a nice chest. And a sexy, older doctor had winked at her!

"Maybe if we all call Lenny, he'll come to us," Zola said. They sat in a circle on the floor and held hands.

"Okay, now, concentrate," Min said.

"One, two, three, *Lenny,*" they yelled in unison. It wasn't a full-out yell because Min's parents were upstairs, but it was still pretty forceful.

Nothing happened. "Wait," Zola said. "Maybe we should make him an offering."

"You mean like a sacrifice?" Sally asked.

"We could kill that," Min said, pointing to the vacuum cleaner cozy.

"What is that?" Olivia asked. "I've always wondered."

Min just rolled her eyes in response. "You don't want to know."

"I bought Lenny a present. We can give it to him from all of us," Zola said.

"What is it?" Sally asked, feeling slightly annoyed. She hadn't bought Lenny a present, and she was sort of his favorite. Why was Zola kissing up to Lenny behind everyone's back?

"It's a cool pair of boxer shorts," Zola said.

"I think he probably wears briefs," Min said. "Who wears boxers under leather pants?"

"How much did they cost?" Sally asked.

"Ten dollars," Zola said.

"Ten dollars?" Sally said. "If all four of us give it to him, that's only two dollars and fifty cents each. That's not much of a sacrificial offering."

"It's the thought that counts," Olivia said. "I think it's worth a shot."

Zola got the gift box out of her overnight bag and put it in the middle of the circle.

"I think someone should hold it up in the air," Olivia said.

"Who gets to hold it?" Sally asked.

"Zola can hold it because she bought it," Olivia said.

"But it's from all of us," Sally said.

"Min should hold it because it's her party," Zola said.

Min took the box from the center and held it high above her head and looked up to the heavens. "Okay, now concentrate," she said. "One, two, three, *Lenny,*" they yelled.

Nothing happened again.

"I think we should call him Clarence," Sally said. "He's probably not coming because we're calling him Lenny."

"All right, let's try again," Min said. "My arms are getting tired holding this dumb present. Ready? One, two, three, *Clarence,*" they all yelled.

And finally, he appeared.

"You rang?" he said, trying to sound annoyed, but he was really enjoying the whole thing immensely.

"We have something for you," Zola said.

Why does she get to tell him? Sally wondered. "It's from all of us," she told Clarence.

Min handed Clarence the You're the Man box and he opened it gingerly. He held up the motorcycle boxer shorts and felt suddenly overwhelmed with emotion. His eyes welled up with tears like Sally Field at the Academy Awards. They liked him. They really liked him.

This was highly unusual in the fairy godmother business. The fairy godmother never *got* anything. You didn't exactly see Cinderella at the ball stuffing pastries in her purse to bring back to her fairy godmother. No, Cinderella wasn't out shopping for boxer shorts with her own money.

"What's the occasion?" he asked, with false modesty.

The girls looked at each other, wondering how to tell him that they needed more help.

"It's a belated Mother's Day present," Olivia said.

"Well, thank you, kiddies," he said. "A pair of You're the Man boxer shorts is the perfect Mother's Day present for a great fairy godmother such as myself." He cut himself a piece of cake and took a bite. "Mmmm. I'm in the best mood now."

"Well, good," Zola said. "You really deserve it."

"Yeah," Sally said. "You're the best fairy godmother in the whole world."

"Here, sit down and relax," Min said, fluffing up one of the couch cushions and handing Clarence the remote control to the television. "Make yourself at home. Is there anything I can get for you?"

"A Coca-Cola would be nice," Clarence said.

Min ran upstairs and brought down a bottle of Coke and a stack of plastic cups. She poured a glass for Clarence.

"This is as flat as a five-year-old," he said.

"Sorry," Min said. "Do you want me to go to the store?"

Olivia cut him another piece of cake and put it on the coffee table. "In case you want seconds."

Suddenly Clarence caught on. This wasn't the warm, cozy love fest he thought it was. Let's face it, teenage girls spent their money on certain things. Themselves. They did not spend their allowances on boxer shorts for others, even if the boxer shorts weren't exactly pricey, unless they wanted something. And that's exactly what they wanted—something.

"I think what we've got here is four little kiss-assers," Clarence said, taking a bite of his second piece of cake. "Ass kissers, *n'est-ce pas?*"

"You're so cynical!" Zola exclaimed. "Maybe we just wanted to do something nice for you."

"Cynical? Me?" Clarence said. He put his feet up on the coffee table, clicked on the television, and started flipping channels.

(Dog Show)

Clarence settled on the Westminster dog show. It was the small-dog category, and strange-looking people were trotting their poofed-up dogs around the ring at Madison Square Garden. You could tell the little dogs thought they were big, the way they strutted with their tails up in the air.

"The best thing about little dogs like that is that they keep the sidewalks clean," Clarence said. "They're like walking dust mops."

A long-haired dachshund circled the ring, followed by a long-haired skinny man in a seersucker suit. Then there was a fat white pug being led by a short, fat, scrunch-faced woman. A shaggy Tibetan terrier pranced ecstatically on the leash of his owner, a man with a shaggy beard that stuck out from the end of his chin.

"This is making me think of Ozzy," Min said. "Can we put something else on, please?"

"It's boring," Olivia said. "Who cares about dogs?"

"Some people really get into it," Zola said.

"You mean some freaks really get into it," Min said. "Really loving your dog like Tobias does is one thing, but breeding them and parading them around like that is a different story."

"Would anyone mind if I enjoy the dog show in peace and quiet?" Clarence asked. "And besides, judge not others lest others should judge you." He knew that wasn't exactly the correct expression, but he was on a bit of a sugar high from the cake and he wasn't thinking completely clearly.

On the TV screen a Yorkshire terrier got ready to strut his stuff.

"Ooh, looook," Min said. "Isn't that the cutest thing you ever saw in your life?"

"I'm glad you think it's so cute, Min," Clarence said.

"Why?" she asked.

"Did you happen to notice who is accompanying that Ozzy look-alike around the stage?" Min looked at the fat woman beside the Yorkie. It was her.

"Oh no," Min said, putting her face in her hands. "I'm fat again?"

The following information appeared on the screen. *Name: L'il Tobi; Breed: Yorkshire Terrier; Breeder: Min Weinstock Frank.*

"I become a professional breeder?" Min asked.

"Don't be so depressed, Min," Clarence said. "You may be fat, but L'il Tobi is about to win Best in Show. Congratulations!"

Min watched her fat self get interviewed by a reporter. "How did you get interested in Yorkshire terriers?" he asked.

"It all started with my little Ozzy angel," the future Min said. She had a slightly crazed look in her eyes, and her hair looked all raggedy as if she hadn't had it professionally done in years. She probably combed it with a dog brush. "My husband and I live in rural Wisconsin. We currently have thirty-seven Yorkies, and we love each and every one of them. Their names are Piggyback, Big Mama, Little Lady, Sneezy, Clementine, Zola, Olivia, Sally . . ."

The interviewer pulled the microphone away from her before she could list all thirty-seven names. "Uh, how does it feel to be the big winner here this evening?" he asked.

"Well," Min said, "we're thrilled to win Best in Show here in New York City or, as we like to call it, New *Yorkie* City."

Min almost threw up. New Yorkie City? That was her future idea of funny? Thirty-seven Yorkies? This was her future? Her future was all Yorkies?

"All Yorkies all the time," Clarence clarified, reading her mind.

"Thanks a lot," Min said.

"You named dogs after us?" Zola asked. "I don't know how I feel about that."

Unfortunately the interview ended before Min could find out more about herself. Or maybe it was fortunate.

"And that's all for Westminster two thousand eleven," the announcer said.

"Wait," Min said, with a tone of desperation in her voice. She grabbed Clarence's arm. "My last name was Frank. It sounds like I'll still be married to Tobias."

Clarence shrugged.

"But that's impossible!" Min said. "We broke up. We definitely ended things permanently."

"Oh, really?" Clarence said. "I'm afraid nothing is ever permanent. Unless you truly feel it in your heart. Until then, it's very much all up in the air." He looked skyward to emphasize his point. "Things chip away like five-day-old nail polish. Slow songs get released as upbeat techno remix versions like Madonna's 'Don't Cry for Me, Argentina.' Just look at the Fugees. . . ."

"Do you mind if I ask what the hell you're talking about?" Min said, on the verge of tears.

A commercial came on TV for Tide liquid with bleach. "See? Some stains come out, some don't," Clarence said. "All you can do is try your best and know when to send something to the dry cleaner's or when to throw it in the rag bin under the sink. But first you need all the information. You have to gather the data."

"But I don't have enough information," Min said. "All I know is I win Fattest in Show."

"Who sounds cynical now? Tell me this: Did you look happy?" Clarence asked.

"Yeah, I guess I did look pretty happy," Min admitted.

"Well, that's something at least. A small change in the right direction, I'd say. Why don't you try to be a little easier on yourself?"

Right now, though, Min was anything but happy. She didn't know exactly what she wanted the future to look like. But she knew she didn't want it to have four legs, a wet nose, and fur.

"Let's see what else is on the boob tube," Clarence said.

(Court TV)

"I'm sure glad your parents have cable," Clarence said. He watched a few minutes of the Richard Simmons *E! True Hollywood Story* and then switched to Court TV.

"Why are all men like this when it comes to the remote control?" Zola said.

"Hey, what happened to Clarence Terence appreciation day?" Clarence said.

"Sorry," Zola mumbled.

A woman stood on the steps of a courthouse, talking into a Court TV microphone. "Today the knock-down-drag-out divorce case of *Fell v. Fell,* otherwise known as the Revenge Ransack Case, was finally brought to a close. The famed divorce attorney representing Mr. Fell, known for her particularly cutthroat and lengthy cases, was so passionate about this particular case, she admitted to going undercover herself to dig up the dirt on the now ex–Mrs. Fell."

Zola's mouth dropped open.

The reporter continued. "In one of the longest divorce decrees in history, Mr. Fell retained custody of the two children as well as all their property, including two cars and two houses. Rumors persist that Mr. Fell and his sharklike attorney are involved in a little trial of their own. A trial love affair, that is. We hear the attorney always plays it safe, however, and never goes anywhere, even out on a date, without a court stenographer present to record the conversation. This reporter can't help but wonder if she brings a court stenographer with her into the bedroom as well."

"Evan and I have a bitter divorce?" Zola asked, horrified. "That bitch attorney comes along and ruins my marriage to Evan?"

Clarence pointed to the television.

"I think someone is coming out of the courthouse now," the reporter said. She rushed to join the other reporters, who were crowding around a woman walking out of the grand doors of the courthouse.

It was Zola. She was wearing a sleek red Armani suit with a short skirt and stunning matching red Prada shoes. She looked like an ad for successful living.

"Ms. Mitchell, Ms. Mitchell," the reporters said. "Is the defendant at all remorseful that he is taking custody away from his wife?"

The future Zola leaned into the microphone. "What goes around comes around," she said calmly.

"Is it true, Ms. Mitchell, that you bring court stenographers with you on dates?"

"Only the attractive ones," the future Zola said with a wry smile.

Just then Evan came out of the courthouse and pushed through the crowd to get to Zola. Then they walked down the court steps arm in arm, got into a silver Jaguar, and drove away. The license plate on the Jag said ZOLAW.

"Former bathing suit model Zola Mitchell, ladies and gentlemen. Now the winner of one of the most widely talked about divorce cases in the state of California."

"I'm the attorney?" she asked, completely incredulous.

"Divorce attorney. Clawed your way to the top. Will stop at nothing to win a case. Prenuptial agreements start being called Zolas after you. Men say to their fiancées, 'Before we get married, honey, I have to ask you to sign a Zola.'"

Zola was speechless.

"Pretty impressive, isn't it?" Clarence said. "I guess all your sneaky, cutthroat, borderline-criminal, obnoxious behavior of the past twenty-four hours has really paid off. And you sure know how to dress," he said.

"This is amazing!" Zola said. "I get Evan in the end! And it looks like we live in LA!"

Clarence shrugged.

"So was Evan still married to that bitch Claudia?" Zola asked.

Clarence pointed to the screen and a red-eyed, sniveling Claudia Choney came wobbling out of the courthouse. She looked frail and tired. Her hair hung in her eyes.

The reporters swarmed around her. "Mrs. Fell, how does it feel? Married to your high school sweetheart, king and queen of your high school prom, and it all ends here today."

"I will hate Zola Mitchell until the day I die," Claudia swore bitterly into the television camera.

"Ha!" Zola shouted triumphantly. "Eat shit and die!"

Clarence just shook his head.

Olivia was watching the whole thing wide-eyed. This wasn't exactly your typical quiet night at home watching television. This was serious. And she had a feeling she was up next on tonight's scheduled programming. She was actually feeling a tiny bit optimistic. At least she wasn't going to be a stewardess anymore.

She grabbed a couch pillow and put it on her lap, holding on to it like a flotation device.

Again Clarence Terence flipped through the channels. This time he paused at the *Ricki Lake* show. But Ricki didn't look like herself. She was rail thin. She looked like she had lost about a hundred pounds. The topic was: Flight Attendants Who *Lay* Over in More Ways Than One.

"Oh no," Olivia said.

"It could be worse," Clarence said. "You could be on *Jerry Springer.*"

"Our producers have prepared a little video footage to

show us what Olivia's daily life as a flight attendant is like," Skinny Ricki said. "Roll the tape."

"Hi, I'm Olivia, and this is what it's like working as a flight attendant on an airplane," the future Olivia said into a camera.

Olivia looked at herself on TV. There was something different about her, but she couldn't quite figure out what it was.

"It's time for the dinner service," the future Olivia said. She wheeled the cart down the aisle. "Would you like healthy heart chili or mini-muffin pizzettes? All right, sir, one healthy heart chili. And for you, ma'am? Healthy heart chili or mini-muffin pizzettes? Healthy heart chili for you, too? All righty! Would you care to join us for some healthy heart chili or mini-muffin pizzettes? We have mini-muffin pizzettes and healthy heart chili on the menu this evening."

Olivia sat on the couch, cringing, as she watched herself serve the trays of disgusting food. Her future had gotten worse, not better. She now said things like "all righty"!

"At least you're not serving chicken thumbs, like last time," Clarence said. "I almost threw up watching you do that."

"So nothing has changed?" Olivia said.

"Well, I wouldn't say that. There's one major difference I can see."

"What?" Olivia asked. She looked different. Good. But not as good as Zola had, that was for sure.

"You really don't see anything different about yourself?" Clarence prodded.

The future Olivia was still on the screen serving dinners, but now the video was all sped up in fast motion so she looked like a crazy person zooming all over the place.

"Do you notice anything different about your uniform?" Clarence asked. He was trying to be delicate about this particular matter.

Then Olivia saw what Clarence was talking about. Her breasts were about five sizes bigger! It looked like she had a couple of balloons in her blouse.

"That's it? That's the big change in my future? I get a boob job?"

"Yup, that's the big development, so to speak," Clarence said.

Skinny Ricki came back on. "Wow, all that food is making me hungry. So with all that work, Olivia, you still manage to have time to fool around with more than one man?"

The future Olivia nodded guiltily.

"And now," Skinny Ricki said, "you have come on the show today for a DNA test to find out which one is the real father of your baby."

"I know who the father is," the busty Olivia said.

"But the man you say is the father isn't so sure he is the real father," Skinny Ricki said. "Isn't that right? Should we bring the man who says he might not be the father out onstage?"

The studio audience cheered.

"Whoops, we have to take a commercial break, but we'll be right back to meet the possible father of Olivia's baby and reveal the DNA paternity results."

The music came on and the audience started screaming, "Go, Ricki, go, Ricki," like a bunch of idiots.

Clarence clicked off the television.

"I don't understand," Olivia said. "I always watch these shows and I think, 'What pathetic loser would act like that?' Wouldn't my future get at least a little better since I intend to work harder and write all those colleges I turned down and ask them if I can still come?"

"You intend," Clarence said.

"That's right, Lenny, I intend to do a lot in the next couple of weeks until graduation. I may even be valedictorian."

"You intend," Clarence said again. "I intend to date Jennifer Lopez."

Olivia got his point.

"Good," Clarence said, reading her mind.

Sally was the only one left. She sat in front of the television from hell waiting to see what life was going to dish up for her.

"Would you like another piece of cake?" she asked Clarence. She was trying to think of ways to stall.

"No thank you, three's my limit," Clarence said.

Clarence turned the TV back on and flipped to ABC. A commercial came on for the American Express card. A girl in her late twenties was taking her distinguished-looking gray-haired father out to lunch. The check came and the daughter put her American Express card down on the table. She told her father that she wanted to treat him to lunch for a change.

Sally and Clarence both teared up a little. "Those commercials just kill me," he said, trying to fight back tears.

Sally wished that she was the girl in the commercial.

She wished that commercial was her future. She wished she could be attractive and successful enough to have her own American Express card and take her father out to lunch.

Sally hadn't seen her father in over a year, since he moved out of Wisconsin. She hoped in the future she would have a good enough relationship with him to sit in a restaurant and have a nice lunch.

The commercial ended and *Oprah* came on. The theme song for her show played and Oprah stood on the stage, wearing an enormous gold necklace.

"What is she wearing around her neck?" Sally asked.

"It's an Olympic gold medal," Clarence said.

"Why is Oprah wearing an Olympic gold medal?" Sally asked. She hoped if they talked about Oprah long enough, she could avoid seeing her future altogether.

"She wins the gold in the 2008 Olympics for long-distance running and she wears the medal every day on the show as a symbol of what can be achieved if you put your mind to it. Oprah can do anything," Clarence said, his voice filled with admiration.

"Welcome to my book club," Oprah said.

Sally sat up straight. Lenny had tuned in to Oprah's Book Club? She loved watching Oprah's Book Club. All of a sudden it occurred to Sally that *she* might be on Oprah's Book Club.

"I'm on Oprah's Book Club?" she asked Clarence.

"Yes, I guess you are," he said.

Sally was so excited, she could barely breathe. So, she was a writer! A writer of books. An author. A novelist. And her book had been picked by Oprah Winfrey, which would make her an instant best-seller if she wasn't one already. This was unbelievably fantastic.

"The book we are discussing today is the best book I have ever read," Oprah said. "I love this book so much that I didn't feel that words were enough to describe to the author how much I admire her and how grateful I am to her for having such a huge effect on my life." Oprah fingered the Olympic gold medal around her neck. "So I've decided to give this to the author as a small token of my gratitude because she *is* the gold medal winner of authors."

The audience gasped.

Oprah took the medal off from around her neck.

Sally could not believe that in just a moment Oprah was going to give her the medal.

The camera panned the applauding audience, and there in the front row was Sally. It was a terrible shot of her. She was sneezing and wiping her nose with the back of her hand. She was wearing a frumpy turtleneck and baggy pants. She looked awful.

If she was the author, what was she doing in the

audience? she wondered. And why hadn't she bothered to put on any makeup or wear a nice suit or dress?

Then a statuesque young woman came on the screen and Oprah put the gold medal around her neck.

People in the audience started standing up one at a time and asking the author questions and giving comments about the book.

The future Sally stood up in the audience and spoke into the microphone. "Ms. Bicks, I just had to come here today and tell you how much I loved your book. I took the day off to drive to Chicago to tell you that. You've been such an inspiration to me."

"Thank you," the author said. "Are you a writer, too?" the author asked future Sally.

Sally sat on the couch next to Clarence and held her breath. Well, was she?

"Not really," future Sally said, shrugging.

For a moment Sally was horribly disappointed, but then she realized she had said not *really*. So maybe she was a little bit of a writer, at least.

"What do you do?" the author asked future Sally kindly.

"I'm a guidance counselor in a high school, and your book has really meant a lot to me and all the great kids there." She looked right into the camera. "I'd like to say hi to all my kids at La Follette High School in Madison. Hi, kids!"

"I'm still a high school teacher?" Sally asked Clarence.

"No, not a teacher," Clarence said. "A guidance counselor. I guess it's all those books you're reading. People feel comfortable enough around you to really open up and talk. That's not really so bad, is it?"

"Yes, it is," Sally said. "I want *men* to feel comfortable enough with me to open up and talk. Not kids. Not dumb La Follette High School kids."

"Well, what can I tell you?" Clarence said. "That's the way the cookie crumbles."

"Thanks so much for the helpful words of wisdom. What's your future, Lenny?" Sally snapped. "Wordsmith-poet-philosopher?"

"All I'm saying is if you want to be a published writer, you'll probably have to actually write something somewhere other than your diary," Clarence said. "And my name is Clarence, although I wouldn't mind if you wrote a character after me and named him Lenny. I've actually been written about by many great writers. In fact, some great writers consider me their muse."

Light started to come through the basement window. It was almost time to go to school again. The American flag waved proudly on the TV screen as the "Star-Spangled Banner" played.

The girls couldn't keep their eyes open for another minute. Clarence clicked off the television and they fell asleep right where they were on the sofa.

26

(Playing Hooky)

The girls couldn't very well go to school. They had such dark circles under their eyes, they looked like professional football players with coal smeared on their faces.

Sally couldn't face everyone after the humiliation in the self-defense assembly. Olivia hadn't written her paper after all, and it wasn't really worth going to school without it. Min was worried that Myles or Tobias would come looking for her at school, and she just couldn't face either of them right now. And Zola was worried that the grade changes would be discovered, especially now that Olivia wasn't turning in her paper.

There was only one thing to do: cut.

And there was one place they loved to do it: the Madison zoo.

"Just as long as we don't see any dogs there," Min said.

"There might be some prairie dogs," Zola said.

The first stop after paying admission was the reptile house. Zola, Min, and Olivia all went inside, and Sally sat outside on a bench as usual. Nothing would make her go in there. She did not see any appeal in walking around a dark building that was filled with huge disgusting snakes. Across the zoo was a newborn giraffe. The fact that Zola, Olivia, and Min would rather see lizards and snakes than an adorable new baby giraffe made her wonder about her choice of friends.

Sally took out her journal through force of habit and wrote the date in the top-right-hand corner. She was about to write a sentence about being at the zoo, on a bench, et cetera, but she stopped herself before her pen hit the page. Instead she wrote the words, *Chapter one. Have you ever thought about your future?* It was the first sentence of her novel.

"Hey, Sally," Zola said, coming up behind her with Olivia and Min right behind her.

"Where should we go next?" Min asked.

"Monkeys!" they all said at once. It was the one thing all four of them could always agree on. They loved to watch the monkeys and name each one after the different boys at their school.

On the way they passed a woman dressed as a clown who was painting children's faces.

"Let's do it," Olivia said. "Let's get our faces painted."

Everyone thought it was a hilarious idea. Sally went first.

"What animal do you want to be?" the clown asked.

"Tiger," she said. A tiger was a confident animal. It suited her mood perfectly. The woman painted orange and black stripes on Sally's pale cheeks. She looked more like an Indian warrior than a tiger. An Indian warrior with long black whiskers.

Sally paid the woman five dollars. "Who's going next?" Sally asked.

"Actually I can't do it," Olivia said. "I have that date tonight with Holden."

"But it was your idea in the first place," Sally accused.

"I know, but I don't think I would look too mature showing up with an animal face," Olivia said.

"I don't think I should do it, either," Min said, scrutinizing Sally's stripes. "I might have to talk to Tobias later and it just wouldn't be right to look like I had a great time out with my friends at the zoo with everything going on between us right now."

"That's a good point," Zola said. "None of us should really do it because our parents are going to figure out we cut if they see us with our faces painted like that."

"But *one* of us already did it," Sally said, frustrated. "Why didn't you all think of these things before making me the guinea pig?"

"Not the guinea pig," Zola said. "The tiger. *Grrrrrrrr.*"

"Remind me never to get tattoos with you guys," Sally said.

Everyone laughed except for Sally. It was pretty funny to think of Sally getting a tattoo.

"Now I have to walk around all day looking like a moron," Sally said.

The clown looked insulted.

"Oh, come on, Sally, you look totally cute," Olivia said.

"Yeah," Zola said. "You're definitely going to get a boyfriend looking like that."

They walked over to the monkey cage and watched two monkeys practically having sex. It was obscene.

Sally didn't want to let on how horrified she was. If sex was anything like that, she didn't want anything to do with it.

"That one looks exactly like Claudia Choney," Zola said, pointing to one sitting on a rock, picking her nose with one hand and holding a toy cell phone to her ear with the other hand.

"Hey, Claudia Choney, stop picking your nose," Olivia yelled.

"Actually she's a lot more ladylike than Claudia and a hell of a lot cuter," Zola said.

But then she stopped. Talking about Claudia made her suddenly remember her future from the night before. She had seemed awfully bitter. She was glad she got Evan in the end, but she had seemed like such a horrible, cut-throat person. Zola tried to shake this new bad feeling, but she couldn't. Maybe her future hadn't been as good as she thought it was.

The four girls walked in silence for a while, stopping for Min to get a Fudgsicle because she had seen a little girl eat one at the monkey cage and whenever she saw someone eat something, she suddenly became in the mood for that particular thing.

They stood and watched the seals slip and slither along the rocks in the center of their pool. It was almost time for the two o'clock feeding.

The seals swam around and around in circles, and Zola watched almost in a trance. She was trying to figure something out, but she wasn't sure exactly what it was. Then something occurred to her. It was almost so obvious, she didn't say it out loud for a moment.

"You know," she said finally. "Now that we know about our futures, it's so easy to change them. We've been going to all kinds of trouble for nothing."

"What do you mean?" Sally asked.

"Well, I know I end up a bitter divorce attorney. So, it's simple. I just won't go to law school. I mean, doesn't that make sense? If I don't go to law school, I can't end up a lawyer," Zola said.

"That's true!" Olivia said excitedly. "And I just won't become a flight attendant. No matter what, I won't become a stewardess. Easy. In fact, just in case, I won't ever even get on a plane. I'll only go where I can drive or take a train or a bus. Like Aretha Franklin."

"And I won't get a dog," Min said. "Even though I love dogs," she added sadly.

"I don't know," Sally said. "This sounds a little too easy. I don't think Lenny would go to all this trouble if it was as easy as you're saying."

"But Sally, it makes all the sense in the world. Just make sure you leave Madison after you graduate from college. No matter what, just move away. If you find yourself feeling like you want to become a guidance counselor, just say *no*. If someone offers you tickets to the *Oprah Winfrey Show,* don't take them."

Zola was so excited by her revelation, she felt like she had just solved the mysteries of the universe.

A man came out in a skintight black scuba-diving outfit to feed the seals. It was Clarence Terence, holding a bucket of slimy fish.

"There's just one problem with your theory, Zola," Clarence said, with an amused smile on his face. Whenever he showed people their futures, sooner or later they came up with this brilliant idea.

"What is it?" Zola asked, trembling slightly.

"You're not going to remember," Clarence said.

"Oh, now you're telling me I'm going to get early Alzheimer's or something?" Zola said.

"Just about this," Clarence said. "In a short period of time, I can't tell you exactly how long, maybe a few days, maybe weeks, maybe even a year, you're going to forget all about me. Nothing I have said or shown you will stay in your consciousness."

The girls were speechless.

"Everyone gets a glimpse of his or her future at some point, usually in the teenage years. You girls are particularly lucky. Not everyone gets to actually meet their fairy godmother. And no other fairy godmother has as much . . . *je ne sais quoi* . . . *pizzazz,* let's say, as I do. But no one ever remembers it."

"But I want to remember you, Lenny," Sally said, suddenly in tears.

"Well, I'm afraid you won't. It's not possible. And besides, you can't even remember that my name is not Lenny," Clarence said. "That's why I'm trying to really teach you something. Something to carry with you always. You know, like I'm trying to teach you how to fish instead of just giving you fish."

A seal jumped into the air and grabbed a fish out of his hand.

"I'm trying to teach you how to teach yourselves." He

held out a giant hoop, and one by one the seals jumped through it for their reward. "I'm teaching you how to perform surgery instead of just giving you a Band-Aid and kisses."

"Okay, okay, we get the picture," Zola said. "Why do you always have to be so melodramatic about everything? One thing I won't mind not remembering is your big speeches all the time."

Sally's mind was racing. She couldn't believe that she would wake up one day and not remember Lenny.

"Clarence?" Sally asked, careful not to call him Lenny.

"Yes, Sally," Clarence said before kissing a seal on the snout.

"Does that mean that my parents got to see their futures when they were kids?" Sally asked.

"Yes, they did, Sally," Clarence said gently. It was impossible not to love Sally with her face painted like a little girl. "In fact, Min, I showed you to your father long before your parents even met."

Min, Sally, Olivia, and Zola suddenly became emotional. It was overwhelming to think about all this. They had to change their futures while they still remembered what their futures were. Did that even make sense? It was all too much to think about.

"I shouldn't have told you," Clarence said. Once again, he realized, he had gone too far. Forgotten his boundaries. No matter how hard he worked in his psychoanalysis, he always had trouble with boundaries. "I think what we all need right now is to have a little fun," he announced, changing the subject and hopefully the tone.

The girls looked at him with apprehension. It was always a little bit nerve-racking when Lenny said he wanted to have fun. You never knew when it might involve space travel or something like that.

"How about a swim?"

Before they knew it, the girls had kicked off their shoes and were jumping into the seal pond. The water was cold and refreshing, and they felt young and silly and hysterical and naive and filled with wonder that it was even possible to do what they were doing.

"I've always wanted to swim with the dolphins," Olivia squealed, diving down into the water without even caring if her hair got wet.

"These are seals," Clarence said.

One large seal took a particular interest in Sally. It wouldn't leave her side. She was so busy being careful not to get her face wet, she had barely noticed all the seal attention. Even though she had complained about it, she kind of liked having her face painted like a tiger.

"Hey, Sally, who's your boyfriend?" Zola asked.

"That's Chester," Clarence said.

"Chester the molester," Zola added. "See, Sally, I

told you you'd get a boyfriend with that tiger makeup."

"Actually, Chester's a girl," Clarence said. "But she sure likes Sally."

"Hey, Sally, maybe you're a lesbian," Min said.

Sally froze. First Zola kissed her, then this female seal, and now Min was announcing that Sally was a lesbian.

"I am not a lesbian!" Sally shouted. "Kissing Zola at the prom meant nothing!"

Zola, Min, and Olivia all stopped and stared wide-eyed at Sally. They didn't even know what she was talking about.

Then Zola swam over to her and said, "Oh, darling, you're breaking my heart," really dramatically. "Kiss me, my darling, kiss me." She puckered up her lips. *"Mwa, mwa, mwa."*

It was so funny that Sally started laughing in spite of herself. Then they all started laughing. "No one thinks you're a lesbian, Sally," Zola said when she could stop laughing long enough to speak. "But we can't say the same thing for Chester."

Sally felt so relieved, she flipped over on her back and let Chester the lesbian seal nibble her toes.

They splashed around and then lay on the rocks in the middle of the seal pool to dry off for a while.

"Whatever happens," Sally said, "this has got to be the most fun day of my whole life."

The others agreed.

"Will we remember it?" Min asked Clarence.

"You will always remember swimming today," Clarence said. "You'll remember how much fun it was and how brave you were to climb over the glass wall and jump in. And when you think of it, you will be reminded of how important it is to take risks. The only thing you won't remember is this fine man here with you, if y'all know what I'm sayin'."

The girls smiled at Lenny. They were sorry they wouldn't remember him, but they were glad they would at least have something to hold on to.

Min looked at her watch. "Oh my God," she said, snapping them all back to reality. "I promised Tobias weeks ago that I would get Ozzy and bring him to Doggy Day Care right now. Tobias has his philosophy oral exam and the professor is allergic to dogs. He told Tobias if he brings Ozzy, it's an instant fail."

"Ozzy can stay in the house alone. He doesn't need constant attention," Zola said.

"He hates being alone," Min said.

"I'm sure, after your fight, Tobias probably made other plans for Ozzy," Olivia said. "He can't expect you to take care of him now."

"But I promised," Min said, really upset. "Now he'll *really* hate me."

"Well, it's too late now," Zola said.

"Unless . . . ," Min said, looking pleadingly at Clarence.

"Oh no," Clarence said. "That's going just a little bit too far."

(27)

(Doggy Day Care)

Clarence had to be the biggest sucker ever. Why did he do these things? All the other fairy godmothers were in—show 'em their futures—and out again the same day. But this! This was a new all-time low. Baby-sitting a dog! What would they have him doing next, the laundry?

Well, it was his own fault. Anyone else would have just been able to say no. He must have been the only one who missed out on the whole 1980s Nancy Reagan just-say-no thing.

Clarence walked Ozzy to Doggy Day Care, stopping long enough for Ozzy to make an enormous poop on the sidewalk. The pile of poop was bigger than Ozzy's head.

"You should pick that up," an old lady said, walking by. She pointed her cane at it.

Clarence glared at the old bag.

"You must be feeding her too much," the old woman said.

Everyone was a critic. "She's a he," Clarence said. "And I do not feed him too much."

The old woman stopped walking and just stood looking at the poop on the sidewalk and shaking her head with a disapproving look on her wrinkled old face.

"Okay, show's over," Clarence said.

"I'm going to stand here and watch you clean up that mess," the woman said.

"Fine," Clarence said. "Do you happen to have a plastic bag or something I could use?"

The old woman frowned and rooted through her purse. "Well, I do have this bag, but I hate to waste it. It's a perfectly good one. I've only used it seven times."

It was the kind of baggie you put fruit in at the supermarket. It looked like it was about a hundred years old.

"Well, do you mind if I have it?" Clarence asked.

"I don't know," the woman said. "It's my only one."

"How about if I give you a dollar for it?" Clarence asked. He couldn't even believe he was having this conversation. Ozzy was happily sniffing his own poop pile.

"I don't know," the woman said again. "It's a good bag, and I always like to have one in my possession." She rooted around in her purse again and pulled out another baggie. "Oh, look," she said smugly. "I've another one. I tell you what, Mr. Unprepared Dog Walker, you can have it for one dollar and fifty cents."

Clarence was about ready to strangle her. He reached into his pocket and pulled out two one-dollar bills. The old woman grabbed them and put them carefully away in her purse. She handed him one of the baggies.

"You owe me fifty cents," Clarence said.

"I'm afraid I don't have any change," she said, walking spryly off, with her cane clicking on the pavement.

Clarence scooped the poop and held the bag far out in front of him until they made it to the corner garbage can.

He did not see what Min saw in Ozzy. Clarence was more of a big-dog man. It was hard to feel particularly masculine walking something the size of a hair scrunchie. But it was only a few more blocks to Doggy Day Care.

When they got there, Ozzy's little stubby tail stopped wagging and he splayed himself out on the sidewalk like a tiny bearskin rug. Clarence dragged him into the place and a man behind the desk brought him into the small-dog room.

Clarence watched Ozzy through the special glass partition that was designed so that the mommies and daddies could see the dogs but the dogs couldn't see them. He watched Ozzy curl up sadly in the corner of the room while the other dogs—a couple of toy poodles and a King Charles spaniel—happily sniffed each other's butts. Ozzy looked completely miserable.

"Go ahead, boy, play with your friends," Clarence said.

"He can't hear you," the man behind the desk said. "Ozzy has never been much of a dog's dog. He has always been more of a people dog."

Clarence's heart was breaking. He couldn't stand to watch this for another minute. He opened the door to the small-dog room, and Ozzy ran to him with his little tail vibrating at a million beats per minute. "Okay, okay," Clarence said, putting his leash back on him and walking him outside. Ozzy didn't so much as glance back over his shoulder. He was free!

Clarence walked Ozzy to the park, and they sat on a bench. Clarence scooped Ozzy up and put him on his lap. Ozzy licked Clarence's chin and ear, and Clarence giggled. "You're a good boy," Clarence said, scratching him just above his tail, where he'd seen Tobias scratch him. Then, to make Ozzy extra happy, Clarence showed Ozzy his little doggy future: Ozzy and two of his sons, running and chasing sticks on a sandy Hawaiian beach with Tobias. Not too shabby.

Clarence actually had the slightly crazy thought of going over to Mrs. Greenspan's house and signing up for one of Ozzy and Harriet's puppies.

Then Clarence lay on the grass under a nice big tree with Ozzy lying on his chest, and they took a little nap together.

(Breaking and Entering)

No matter how much fun they were having, Zola, Olivia, Min, and Sally decided they weren't accomplishing much at the zoo. As soon as Lenny left they decided to split up and get a move on with changing their lives.

Zola looked at her watch. It was two-fifteen, and Evan would just be walking into English class. Despite seeing herself as a mean-spirited lawyer known for her creepy detective work, she was still dying to get a look at what Evan had written about her on his computer. She knew that Lenny wouldn't approve, but would it really be so bad if she just did it this one time to find out what Evan was really thinking? Jesus, she felt like she had a little mini-Lenny in an angel suit buzzing around her head like a mosquito and annoying the hell out of her. She didn't have all day to debate the ethics of it. This was her only chance to get her hands on his computer. With Evan at school and Todd, his toad of a brother, at school and his

186

parents at work, Zola could just dig the key to the front door out of the cactus plant on the porch and slip up to Evan's bedroom.

The first thing she thought about doing when she entered Evan's room was to search for porn. He always claimed he didn't have any dirty magazines, but Zola wasn't that naive. She figured all teenage boys had porn hidden somewhere in their rooms.

But Zola stuck to her mission. She walked right over to Evan's computer and turned it on. She already knew his password, so it was going to be easy. She typed in *ZM524*. His password was a combination of her initials and Bob Dylan's birthday, May twenty-fourth, which he always said was the perfect blend of his two favorite things in the world—Dylan and her.

For a moment nothing happened, and Zola held her breath. What if it didn't work? What if he had changed his password to *CC524* instead?

Luckily it worked, and she clicked right onto Evan's journal. She pulled up the last entry. Her heart was pounding. She was terrified.

Today I have band rehearsal after school at Jake's house and Claudia is coming to watch (her idea). It's kind of ironic because I spent so much time trying to get Zola to come but she never wanted to. The guys are really pissed that Claudia's been hanging around and they started calling her the Yoko Ono of the band but she doesn't even really get it. But she's a good girlfriend and it's kind of nice being with her, I guess. It's nice that she's so into me and my music and everything but I feel a little weird about it because I don't even know if it's genuine or not. Actually that's not it. I feel weird because I really miss Zo.

Zola smiled to herself. Evan still loved her. He was still thinking about her. He missed her. She had begun to scroll up when she heard a sound. Someone was in the house. She exited the file and tried to shut down the computer, but she didn't have time. She heard footsteps coming up the stairs. She had no idea what to do.

She pushed some of the clothes and junk away from the floor around Evan's bed and slid under. She lay on her stomach, her heart thumping against the wooden floorboards.

Evan's door opened and someone came in. She held her breath. She saw Evan's Puma sneakers walk past the bed and head straight for the computer.

"Todd, you jerk," he mumbled. She heard him turn the computer off.

Evan sat on his bed and the mattress dipped above her. Zola felt ridiculous lying there. But what she had just read had made her so happy. She should just come out from under the bed and tell him that she loved him. He wouldn't be mad that she was in his room as long as she didn't tell him that she had read his journal.

She could lie next to him on the bed and they could have a good laugh about all of this. Maybe they would even make love.

They had lost their virginity together on this very bed. She had been scared out of her mind, more scared even than she had just been a minute ago when he came into the room, but she hadn't let on. He had pulled off her boots for her and fallen backward on his butt and they had laughed. Then he lay on top of her as usual and they made out, but that time they had both gotten undressed. She knew how much he wanted to do it and then, that day, she finally said it was okay. She had pretended to be so cool about it, but she remembered how her legs shook the whole time. She was glad she had done it then because they loved each other and it hadn't ruined anything.

Now Zola wished she had waited. Even though it was stupid to even think about because you couldn't go back and change the past, she wished they still had their first time ahead of them. So it could be today.

Just as Zola was gathering the courage to slide out from under the bed, Evan's phone rang.

"Hello . . . Hi, Claudia," he said. "Me too, it was really fun."

Zola's heart sank.

"Yeah, it really was a great way to celebrate."

Celebrate what? Zola wondered.

"Claudia Choney, class valedictorian," Evan said. "It must feel amazing."

Zola had to stop herself from gasping. What! How had that happened?

"You are the smartest girl I know," Evan said.

Zola couldn't believe what she was hearing. First of all, it was still hard for her to grasp the idea that Claudia had good enough grades to be at the top of the class. But how could she have been selected valedictorian when Zola had personally changed the grades herself? Now Zola was going to have to come up with a whole new form of revenge.

Evan started to strum his guitar. Zola knew that when he did that while he was talking on the phone, it meant he was distracted.

"What?" he said. "Yeah, I'm listening. Okay, I'm just going to catch a shower and then I'm going over to practice."

He said good-bye to her and hung up. Zola was so mad, it was all she could do to keep herself from reaching her arm out from under the bed and grabbing Evan's sweat-socked ankle as he headed past the bed and out the bedroom door to the bathroom. Zola waited until she heard the shower running for a few minutes. Then she crawled out from under the bed, like some kind of lowly insect, and ran down the stairs and out the door as fast as she could.

(Tiger)

For a few minutes Sally forgot that she had kid's face paint on her face. She had no idea why people were staring at her. She thought it must be her new daring attitude until she caught a glimpse of her reflection in the window at Styx. But by then it was too late; she was already there. All she could do was try to act like it was the hot new thing to do.

Sally walked bravely into Styx, the coolest instrument store in town. Amazing electric guitars hung from the ceiling. Glittery gold ones, bright white, fire-engine red. There were amps and keyboards and a row of drum sets. And cymbals, just like Tobias had described.

Sally couldn't believe how many guys were in there. There must have been six or seven gorgeous guys just walking around looking at stuff. A Jimi Hendrix song was playing, and Sally tried to move a little in time with the music. She was really trying to fit in and look cool.

"Cool," a salesman said, coming over to her and

pointing to her face. "What are you, the Cheshire cat?"

"I'm a tiger," Sally said, immediately regretting it. What a stupid kid thing to say. I'm a tiger.

"Okay, Tony the Tiger, can I help you?"

"How much is a drum set?" Sally asked.

"Which one?" the salesman said.

Sally tried to remember exactly what Tobias had said his set had looked like. "A pearl gray Sluggerland with Zoldigan cymbals," she said, trying to sound like a professional.

"Do you mean Slingerland?" the man asked, smiling.

"Uh, yeah," Sally said. "That was just sort of a joke."

"Are you a drummer?" the man asked.

"I drum a little," Sally said. She had no idea why she had said that. She wanted to run out of the store, but she was right in the middle of talking to this guy. He had long hair tied into a ponytail, and he wore a necklace made out of wooden beads around his neck.

"Well, a Slingerland could run anywhere from nine hundred bucks to three grand," the man said.

"Oh," Sally said. "How much are a set of sticks?"

"A pair of drumsticks?" he said. "About twelve bucks. Hey, dude, you look really familiar to me."

Sally shrugged and crossed her arms over her chest. She had never been called "dude" before.

She tried to change the subject. "I'd like to buy a pair," she said.

"You've already got a pair," he said, looking at her chest.

"Of drumsticks," Sally said.

She followed him to the counter, and he showed her the range of sizes. They ran from skinny to fat. She bought a mediumish pair and paid for them. "I don't need a bag," she said.

"I think I'm going to start painting my face like that," the man said.

As soon as Sally left the store with the drumsticks in her hand she felt like a different person. They were amazingly cool. She put them in her miniknapsack and they stuck out. She walked proudly down the street. The sticks were cooler than any accessory she'd ever owned, cooler than any pair of sunglasses or piece of jewelry.

She couldn't wait to give them to Tobias. If she ever saw him again, that was. She felt terrible about what had happened the night before and how she had helped trick him. She hoped he would let her make it up to him.

(Cinderella)

Olivia went to Hair Today to get her hair done for her date that night with Holden. She had promised herself she would spend more time studying and less time sitting in the chair while Esperenza straightened her hair, but this was an emergency situation.

When she got there, she was informed that Esperenza was home sick. After a brief moment of panic, Olivia asked if there was anyone who would be able to see her. She was usually very loyal to Esperenza, but her hair was all frizzy and fishy from the seal pool.

"We have a new stylist," the woman said. "He's *very* good."

Olivia was given a robe and led to the sink for her hair to be washed. She closed her eyes and felt the hands of the hairdresser massage her scalp with lather. When she opened her eyes she was surprised to see that the guy washing her hair looked an awful lot like Lenny. She must have Lenny on the brain. She closed her eyes again.

"Hi, Olivia," she heard Lenny say.

She opened her eyes. "Lenny! What are you doing here?" she asked.

"What does it look like?"

Clarence Terence rinsed her hair, wrapped it in a towel, and led her to a chair.

"You've got to be kidding," Olivia said. "You are not really going to attempt to blow my hair straight. Are you?"

"Don't worry," Clarence said. "I know what I'm doing. I have sisters."

Olivia was worried. "Come on. I really want to look good tonight. This isn't the time for one of your jokes."

Clarence turned on the hair dryer. "I'm sorry, I can't hear you," he said. He squeezed half a tube of Phytologie relaxing gel into his palm and rubbed it into Olivia's hair. He divided her hair into sections using giant pink clips. Then he took the flat brush and went to work, expertly blowing her hair out section by section.

"So, Min and Myles seem to be getting along well," Clarence said.

"I thought you couldn't hear me. Now you want to talk?" Olivia said.

"Yes, I do," Clarence said. "I'm not sure about this whole Holden thing. I really don't want you going out with him."

"I can't hear you," Olivia said.

"Yes, you can. I thought you were going to hand in your paper today. You know they announced the valedictorian today. And you weren't even at school. Cutters don't get chosen."

"Who cares?" Olivia said. "Are you trying to tell me one stupid paper is going to change my whole life?"

"One bad hookup could change your whole life," Clarence said.

"You just told us today that we should be brave and take risks and now you're telling me to be all careful?" Olivia said, frustrated. "Did Cinderella's fairy godmother start giving her all kinds of warnings about Prince Charming? She didn't start going, 'Now, Cinderella, you know the prince is older than you are and he's a mama's boy and he's a bit of a stalker and you really should just stay home and clean the fireplace.' Tonight I intend to enjoy a cold glass of milk and have a great time. I'll worry about my future tomorrow."

Olivia looked at herself in the mirror. The side Lenny had finished was perfectly straight. Straighter than it had ever been.

"I'll tell you one thing, Lenny. If this whole fairy godmother thing doesn't work out for you, you could really do this hair thing for a living. You're great at it," Olivia said. "Now, if you could only zap me into a beautiful ball gown. Perhaps a Dolce & Gabbana or at least a Betsey Johnson . . ."

"I'll make a deal with you," Clarence said. "I'll whip you up a Betsey Johnson if you leave Holden at midnight."

Olivia weighed her options. Midnight was a little early for a college boy. "No deal," she said.

"Twelve-thirty?" Clarence bargained.

"Okay," Olivia said.

"Go into the bathroom," Clarence said. "I can't do it right in the open."

Olivia got out of the salon chair and went into the bathroom with half of her hair still in clips. A moment later, without feeling a thing, she was wearing a totally adorable pink rosebud Betsey Johnson and Lenny had thrown in a pair of cute high-heeled sandals. Olivia felt special. No one else had gotten an outfit. And it was a great deal because she had to be home by one, anyway, or her parents would kill her. She went back to the chair and Clarence finished the other side of her hair. She looked perfect.

"Am I supposed to tip you?" she asked.

The only thing Min could do that night was lie on her bed with her phone on her stomach, waiting for either Tobias or Myles to call. This whole day had almost been like a time-out from real life. It was almost like it didn't count. But tomorrow she would have to go back to school and life would start again for real.

She knew she should do something instead of just lying there. She was supposed to put the dishes in the dishwasher. She could do a little studying. Her parents were downstairs in the rec room, watching *Who Wants to Be a Millionaire* and she could go down and hang out with them for a while. But one thing she definitely did not want to do was watch TV. She never wanted to watch TV again.

The doorbell rang and Min jumped up off her bed. Maybe it was Myles. She checked her reflection in the mirror and then ran downstairs to answer the door.

But it wasn't Myles. It was Tobias and Ozzy. He was holding a giant garbage bag.

"Hey," he said.

"Hey," she said back.

"I brought you something," he said, shoving the garbage bag at her.

"I already have enough garbage," Min said, smirking.

Tobias looked hurt. "Why don't you look inside?"

Min opened the bag and looked in it warily. For a moment she was worried it was going to be Myles chopped up in a million pieces or something.

She reached in and pulled out a sandwich. "What is this?" she asked.

Tobias looked at the sandwich in its individual baggie. "PB and J," he said. "But there's baloney, salami, and cream cheese and tomato."

The bag was filled with dozens and dozens of sandwiches.

"You said you wanted to feed the homeless or whatever," Tobias said. "You know, do a good deed."

Min couldn't believe it. Tobias was like some kind of idiot savant of love. He knew exactly what to do to get back into her heart.

Ozzy started barking at the garbage bag. "He likes the salami," Tobias said.

"So," Min said. "Do you want to drive over to the shelter and give these out now?"

"Well . . ." Tobias seemed reluctant. He looked at his watch. "You know, there's another half an hour of *Millionaire*. . . ."

Min sighed. Tobias had done a nice thing, and he clearly cared about her, but he hadn't had a complete personality makeover. He was the same old-same old.

"My parents are downstairs in 'your room' watching it right now. Why don't you go down and join them?" she said.

"Thanks, Min," Tobias said, heading for the stairs. He turned around. "What if I go down there and they're, you know, doing it or something?"

Min laughed. "Tobias, you are so gross," she said.

Tobias shrugged as if to say, "But you love me, right?" and kept walking.

Alone with Ozzy, Min sat down on the couch. "I tell you what," she said to the dog. "I'll split one with you." She dug for a salami sandwich on white bread, unwrapped it, and ate it, tearing off small pieces for Ozzy. The Yorkie pressed his little body against her leg and sighed happily. He had really missed her.

Everything was back to normal. But then again, it wasn't. Min wasn't even sure what normal was anymore. All she knew was this couldn't be it, this couldn't be all there was.

As she chewed, Min picked up the newspaper from the coffee table and turned to her horoscope. Virgo. "'Today is the first day of the rest of your life; jump into the water and play,'" she read.

"Clarence Terence must write these things," Min told Ozzy. "It sounds just like him."

At exactly the same time, in their different locations, Zola, an Aquarius, Olivia, a Pisces, and Sally, a Leo, picked up a newspaper or a magazine and read their horoscopes. Each one read the same line and smiled. "Lenny," they said to themselves. "Lenny."

Min got up to head out to the shelter alone. She put the newspaper down on the floor next to her. And Ozzy, like the good little dog that he was, jumped down off the couch and peed on it.